David Christie-Murray

A Life's Atonement

David Christie-Murray

A Life's Atonement

ISBN/EAN: 9783741123269

Manufactured in Europe, USA, Canada, Australia, Japa

Cover: Foto ©Andreas Hilbeck / pixelio.de

Manufactured and distributed by brebook publishing software
(www.brebook.com)

David Christie-Murray

A Life's Atonement

A LIFE'S ATONEMENT

A NOVEL

BY

DAVID CHRISTIE MURRAY

AUTHOR OF 'JOSEPH'S COAT' ETC.

IN THREE VOLUMES — VOL. III.

SECOND EDITION

London

CHATTO & WINDUS, PICCADILLY

1881

A LIFE'S ATONEMENT.

CHAPTER I.

HISTORY.

The cruel road seems lovable, though the feet bleed and are weary.

THERE are many places in London where the struggle of poverty for its daily bread is visible to the eye of the most careless wayfarer. But there are not many places where the simile of a fight for life is so palpably true as it is at the gates of some of the London Docks, twice a-day. At almost any of the docks, you may see this strange conflict at early morning, or at the close of the time set apart for the mid-day meal. Round the closed gates are gathered some scores of men

in rough working-dress, who lounge about
with their hands in their pockets, kicking the
pebbles on the highway in a listless fashion ;
or leaning in listless fashion against the gate
or the walls ; or standing listlessly, with
humped shoulders, on the kerb-stone, spitting
at a mark on the road.   They are for the most
part sturdy fellows, with a general aspect of
uneasy massiveness ; an aspect strengthened
by the cut and weight of their loose clothing.
Suddenly the incurious traveller who observes
these things is startled by a yell in which many
voices mingle, and the lounging crowd is
thrown into a state of mad activity.   Everybody converges to one point, and there is a
fight to get there.   At that point a head
and shoulders appear above the high dock-
wall, and a hand showers down a little
snow-storm of limp tickets.   The snow-storm
lasts for a second or two only, and every man
in the crowd fights for a flake of it, for dear
life.   Like other flakes, it will melt in his
hand, though somewhat more slowly than the
common, since it will at least last until meat
and drink are found.   The scrambling fight
goes on until the last ticket is rescued from the
dust or mud.   The winners in the fight range

themselves outside the dock-gates; the losers subsiding suddenly from their heat of passion, lounge again as listlessly as ever; and the two who have torn a ticket between them toss up for it, or bargain for it, or fight for it, as chance or their nature may determine. The small gate within the large one being opened, the winners go in, and are allowed to work; and the losers hang about outside on the chance of being wanted in the course of the morning or afternoon. And by this conflict, twice renewed daily, men earn the right to earn their bread in the capital city of the world's most prosperous empire.

Two days' rest had restored Frank to something of his old strength, and had left him penniless. For a shilling and a halfpenny, husbanded never so carefully, will not find food for any length of time in London. On the morning of the third day he arose, and wandered into the street before the faintest light of dawn had touched the sky. With returning strength came appetite; and before he had gone far he pulled from his coat-pocket the heel of a loaf saved from last night's meal, and munched it as he went. His mind had not lost the power to grasp, but he had lost

the will ; and all mental outlines were dim and
clouded to him.   Hardship in itself is not so
pitiable a thing.   It is the feeling in a man's
mind that he suffers hardship which crushes
and kills.   The young athletes of the Thames
every year challenge discomfort with joyful
hearts, and flourish in it, and go back to the
routine of business or professional strife, made
strong by it.   But, if they faced the same dis-
comforts—light as they are, when compared
to those of poverty — with spirits already
broken by the insupportable burden of fruit-
less hope, the very things that bring health
might carry death with them.   As for Frank,
he had borne the chief agony of his remorse,
and a dull rest which had no sense of rest in
it had taken the place of pain.   It was rather
that the passion of his grief had wept itself to
sleep, than that Peace had as yet even touched
him with one feather of her healing wings.
But if he had not the jocundity of spirit which
makes hardship pleasureable, he had at least
a careless contempt for it, which made it a
thing of no moment to him.   He was in the
wilderness, with no land of promise in sight,
even for the soul's eyes ; but he had no longings after the flesh-pots of lost Egypt.   He

scarcely went back to his old life, in thought, at this time; and whatever change went on within him, whatever process of gathering strength, whatever growth in duty, was uncon- scious. Creeds shift and change, and the light fades here and flashes there in broken gleams on nebulous faiths and hopes which are not steadfast. But in their midst stands one rock solid and fast-rooted, and he who sets his foot thereon is blest even though he be not happy. The name of that rock is Duty, and who walks the harsh and difficult way which lies along it, gathers no clogging load from quagmire, dies no soul's death by the miasma of that murky world which swelters down below it. We slip, we fall, we bemire ourselves, we choke in the deadly fog; but to the sincere soul the hand of guidance comes, and the weak feet find a standing-place again, and the cruel road seems lovable, though the feet bleed and are weary.

It was a dim sense of Duty which left death by starvation in its budget of obvious chances, yet threw suicide out of it. But it was something; and the light broadened above the head and about the feet of this forlornest soul, and lo! the firm eternal rock

was there beneath him, and the way was
clear.

Frank walked, vacuous and unobservant, as
the day grew.　The twilight was chill and
faint, and the wind swept in shivering gusts
along the line of street lamps and the little
pools of water in the road.　He had travelled
altogether out of his knowledge of London,
taking no note of the unaccustomed streets.
There were few signs of life in them, and the
steps of here and there a solitary workman
sounded with a strange and melancholy dis-
tinctness.　But at length the road he took
brought him to a high brick wall, into the
colour of which the smoke of myriads of
chimneys had entered—a desolate, bleak, black
wall which stretched as far as he could see
along the lonely road.　Rounding the corner
of this wall, he saw before him a small
mob of men, who lounged with lazy shoulders at the roadside, or propped themselves
against the wall, or talked in uninterested
knots with each other.　Whilst he noticed
them in that vague way which had now
become habitual with him, he was startled into
interest by a simultaneous shout from half the
unoccupied assembly; and almost before he

had time to ask himself what this might mean,
the men before him were tied in one great
knot of struggling legs and arms. He walked
on faster than before, and reached the place
just as the crowd dissolved of its own accord,
and melted back to its own elements. Though
he did not yet know the reason of the struggle,
he could single out at a glance those who had
won and those who had not won. The former
were full of alacrity, and moved with a definite
step, like men who had got what they wanted
and knew what to do with it. The others fell
back into the old lounge, or moved irresolutely
from side to side of the road, and were evi-
dently undecided as to whether they should go
or stay. Whilst Frank stood still to see what
would come of it all, a heavy hand came down
upon his shoulder, and a hoarse voice with a
chuckle in it cried, ' Hillo ! shipmet. Want
a day's turn at work ? Eh ?'

Frank nodded.

'You look as if you did,' said the man
with the hoarse voice. He was a red-faced,
bright-eyed fellow, past middle age, and had
a grizzled beard of a fortnight's growth. He
stood something over six feet high, and his
shoulders were broad and square. He had on

a sou'-wester, and big sea-boots very much the worse for wear; and his great arms and chest showed their swelling muscles through a tight-fitting grey jersey. 'I've picked up two tickets,' he said, 'and you're welcome to one of 'em.' Two or three of the unsuccessful loungers stood staring hungrily at Frank's new acquaintance; but when they saw him hand over the little ticket, they drew back with disappointed looks, and joined the scattered throng in the road.

Frank had no notion as to the nature of the work or the character of the pay; but he ranged himself beside the man who had befriended him, and when the little gate opened, followed his companion through it. They were employed in ordinary dock-labour, and were kept at it until noon, when they were paid and dismissed. Frank had no fear of labour; but he was unused to it, and was not altogether grieved when he failed to secure a ticket in the afternoon's scramble. The pay was poor, but it was better than nothing; and Frank was on the ground early next morning. As fortune had it, the shower fell about him as he stood a little apart from the rest, and he secured two tickets. Looking round he saw that the man who had helped him the day before was going away; and bethinking him of that good turn, ran after the burly figure.

'One good turn deserves another,' said Frank. 'I have two tickets.'

'You're the right sort,' said the Dockman with an oath, to make the statement more emphatic. 'Half these dogs ud kick your heart out as lief as look at you, even if you saved 'em from starving a day before.'

All that morning he worked alongside Frank and lightened labour for him; but by midday the unaccustomed muscles were tired and stiff again, and Frank was glad to betake him to Bolter's Rents before nightfall. He walked on calmly enough, until he reached the boundaries of his old haunts, and there his heart began to beat with the fear of recognition. He bent his head and slouched along, determined to give as little chance to any scrutiny as possible; and as he walked, he thought how necessary it would be to get lodgings out of the way of his friends, if he meant to live in London. I do not know if I have yet made this clear, that Frank Fairholt's sole dread was that a further sorrow might fall on those whom he had so much wronged already. If it had been possible to surrender himself to justice and to suffer the penalty of his misdeeds without their knowledge, he would even have rejoiced so to quiet his conscience. Therefore he dreaded detection, not for his sake, but for theirs. It is not easy to see how any wretchedness could have added one pang to his sorrows. Walking along, bent on nothing so much as escaping without notice, and feeling that now and again the eyes of passers-by were upon him, and knowing what a blot on the spring sunlight he must look, as he crept through the streets, he heard his own name mentioned by a familiar voice. Those genial young people the Messrs. Brooks and Bonder were at his elbow, and were talking of him. His heart almost stood still; but he bent his head yet lower, and they passed him by unnoticed.

'Poor Fairholt!' one said. 'What has become of him, I wonder?'

'I think he went to the bad about Tasker's business, and bolted somewhere,' said the other.

'Hastings has been spending money like water, trying to find him.'

With that they went on out of hearing,
and a new dread arose in the listener's mind.
It gave him an impulse, and he began to
make an effort to see and understand. He
reached his lodging, and sat down alone to
think. What were the chances of detection,
and what would come of it ? It was clear
that Frank Fairholt and the crime of
Spaniard's Lane were not associated, or Hastings would not be hunting for him, and
Brooks and Bonder would have had some
inkling of it. If it were true that his friends
were seeking him—and that he could not
doubt—they were striving to restore him to
his old place in the world. From the life-
long hypocrisy and horror involved in such
a restoration, he shrank back appalled ; and
rising from his seat, he paced to and fro
along the crazy floor, turning over in his
mind the chances of escape. 'Here in London,' he thought—'I am safer than I could
be elsewhere.' Who could look for him, he
thought, contrasting what he was with what
he had been, in such a den as this ? What
better hope of escape could he find from that
inexorable love, which was harder to bear
than any severity of punishment, with which

he now felt sure some of his old friends would
pursue him? Remembering how Maud's uncle
loved her, it came into his mind that Hastings had received from him the money he
was said to be so lavishly spending, and he
trembled as he thought how far Maud's love
might follow him. The image of her tenderness, the thought of the heart-breaking
sorrow and anxiety he knew she bore, the
place he dwelt in, the clothes he wore, the
life he lived, the black secret that lay hidden
in his own soul, love, remorse, self-loathing,
the hideous prospect of his life—all these were
in his mind, and tore him with unutterable
anguish. How sweet seemed the quiet of the
grave! How the chill voice the river's waters
uttered as they lapped against their oozy banks
called to him! No, no, no! Not that! He
cast out his hands in resolute refusal of that
drear enticement, as the voiceless words shaped
themselves within him. Then a thought came
to strengthen his resolve. 'If I were hunting,' he said within himself, 'for anyone
I cared for, who had vanished out of life
as I have, I should look for suicides.
What if that dread is in their minds,
and they should find their search rewarded

there !' And the Water-Siren beckoned no
more.

He kept his place till dark, and then stole
out for food. In the darkness before dawn
he set out for the scene of his chance labours ;
and failing, hung about till noon ; and failing
again, lounged there still until night came on,
and under the shelter of its gloom stole
home. It was a hard life ; but it held body
and soul together, if by a most uncertain tie ;
and since nothing else opened, he stuck to it.
As he became inured to the labour, his daily
fatigue decreased ; but that was scarcely a
thing to be thankful for. His broad-built
acquaintance, who answered to the impro-
bable name of Gorridge, stuck to him with
great faithfulness ; and the two entered into
a sort of unspoken compact to supply each
other's failing in the fight for tickets, whenever occasion offered. Frank bethought him
often that he might avoid the familiar parts
of the town, and the risk of detection which
attended his travels through them ; but the
solitude he generally secured at Bolter's Rents
made the place more easily endurable than
any other. As time went on, his clothes by
small additions here and there began to as-

sume a heavy long-shore look; and his hair
and beard were rapidly whitening, whether
with suffering, or from purely physical causes.
After a month or two, a change came
over his life, and the coarse employment
he had fallen upon became secured to
him.   The man whose business it was to
distribute the tickets took a fancy to this
grey, quiet, inoffensive Dockman, who was
always to be depended on, who never squab-
bled, never drank, never shirked his work, and
who now began to go about his business with
an air of sense and aptitude which the rougher
and stronger had no chance to reach to.   So
whenever Frank was thrown out in the scrim-
mage, which was not very often, since the dis-
tributor meant to help him, it came to pass
that another man was wanted, and he was
called in.   His needs were so few that eighteen-
pence a-day supplied them; and the residue
of his poor earnings anybody in want was
welcome to.   This was the sacrifice to which
he set himself—to live among these people,
and do his duty as one of them, and to help
such of them as stood in need.   It came about
that after a while the rough fellows got to
know him, and seeing how his money was

mainly spent, forebore to envy the favouritism
shown by the ganger; and some of the set
whom he had helped in times of especial hardship, would have belaboured any who dared
to offer him an insult. It got about somehow—for he never spoke a word concerning
it—that he had a special dislike to the
vile blasphemies which seasoned their common talk; and though they were as coarse
and hard a set as might be found in London,
they were contented after a time to let
their conversation go without that gruesome
flavour.

In his old life, Frank had been remarkable
for the sweet clearness and manly delicacy of
his speech. The accent of an English gentleman is not a thing to be acquired by a dock
labourer, and it is not easily mistakable. He
had never given a thought to the rare beauty
of his own speech. He was unconscious of
that gift of nature and breeding, and so made
no attempt to hide it. It went with his blameless conduct, and his unfailing industry, and
his open-handed generosity, to make him
noticeable in that rough crowd, and they conferred upon him the name of ' The Duke,' half
in genuine admiration, and half in satire.

When it happened, as it sometimes did, that Frank found himself addressed by any of those in authority, his speech surprised them ; and there were legends about him among the clerks, one of which was that he had been worth half-a million, and had lost it, every penny, on three successive Derbies. Had he known these things, they would have re-awakened the fears that slumbered in him, and he would have left the place and returned no more ; but he knew nothing except that the inward burden was no lighter, whilst the outside burden seemed too light to think of.

Under these conditions, his bodily health returned, and his native dexterity made him more than a match at his work for those who were vastly stronger. Meantime, there came even to his ears the news of a great war. The recruiting sergeant became a common figure at the dock-gates at mid-day, and Frank had longings to be out in the Crimea, where, haply, Fate might be good to him and give the only thing it had to give—an unknown grave. But his grey beard made the recruiting sergeant laugh at his proposal to enlist, and he went back quietly to his work again. The sergeant might well be excused, for the grey beard and wrinkled face doubled the applicant's apparent age, and Frank passed commonly amongst those who knew him for a man of fifty, or five-and-forty at the least. Sundays were the days on which his inward burden seemed heaviest, for he dared not leave the house to wander in the streets, safe as he might have been, and the hours were leaden-footed. But one day he picked up a scrap of pencil in the docks, and absently put it in his pocket. Finding it there next Sunday, he began to sketch upon the dingy whitewash of the wall, and growing interested in the task, wore the pencil down to a stump, sharpening it roughly with an old table-knife, the back of which was keener than the edge. He was a born artist, and the passion awaking again within him, he took to saving all manner of scraps of paper, and bearing them home with him. There on Sundays he would sketch all day, for Penk-ridge was generally absent, and at night would burn his work carefully, lest any of it should by any chance get abroad and betray him. Many faces of old friends, many scenes in which he had been happy, his busy pencil traced as he sat alone ; and many a time his eyes were too full of tears to see the lines he had drawn.

The habit took such a hold upon him anew, as abandoned habits will when re-assumed, that he caught himself sometimes in lonely corners at the docks in disengaged moments sketching on the walls, on fragments of board, on anything, with any bit of char-coal or chalk that came to his fingers. There was a certain English official there, who for some occult reason had an ambition to pass for a Yankee, and always spoke through his nose, in transparently unsuccessful imitation of the American twang. This man's face was in Frank's mind, and somehow went from his mind into his fingers, which conveyed it through the medium of a piece of chalk to the top of a tea-chest. It was an absolute likeness; and when the man came that way and saw it, he stared in amaze.

'Come yer,' said he to a passing clerk from the Customs. 'What do you think o' that?'

The clerk laughed, and said it was an amazing likeness.

'Now,' said the depicted one, in nasal fol-lowing of the typical down-Easter of the British stage, 'who could 'a done that thar? Ain't it like? Why, dern me, if I didn't think I'd

took a white outline and got spread out on
that old tea-chest. Petrified fact. I did.'

The official did little else that day but march
up to the tea-chest with newly-caught friends
and acquaintances, to whom he displayed the
outline with the same unvarying formula. No
man with whom the official had the slightest
acquaintance went through the yard free of
that joke, until in the course of the evening
the tea-chest was removed. Frank was at
work in the neighbourhood, and overheard it
half-a-dozen times; but it carried no merri
ment to him, though every one to whom it
was offered was complaisant enough to smile
at it. It awoke anew his dread of discovery,
and he thought, 'I must do no more sketching here. It would surely be too strange a
thing to find an artist in a place like mine,
to pass without some comment or suspicion.'
He kept watch upon his fingers after this;
and in Bolter's Rents he still burned his
Sunday's work with rigid care. The inhabitants of that doleful region saw but little
of him, and for a long time his evident desire for solitude was humoured to the full.
He learned from Penkridge occasional news
of the doings of the place, which otherwise

would not have reached him. He relieved
that broken creature's necessities at times;
and once or twice bestowed some charity
upon the neediest, where all were needy.
Very often his companion talked to him for
an hour together on his return from the
docks; and Frank sitting stock-still, heard
scarce a word, but murmured mechanically
Ay and Yes and No.

One evening he sat thus; and Penkridge's
talk gurgled on unnoticed till the current of
Frank's thought suddenly ran silent, and his
companion's voice went on to this effect:
'Which she's a regular angel, if you'll believe me, sir. It isn't what she gives, though
I do assure you as that's quite considerable;
but it's how she gives it. Many's the 'elping
'and she's lent me sence I've been brought
so low; and many's the 'elping 'and as 'er
'usband lent my poor dear pardner.'

'Ay,' said Frank, not caring whose praises
were thus spoken; and turning to the dingy
window, he looked out upon the night, where
for once the moonlight laid a sanctifying hand
upon the squalors of Bolter's Rents. For the
pure light of the moon seems only to rest on
beauty, and makes ugliness lovely when it

beholds it; as the light of a kindly spirit lays a kindly glow on the hard world, or as love beautifies that which it loves. And for a while the laden heart rested itself upon beauty, and Frank's thoughts roamed sadly, but without anguish, into the autumn fields. He came back from his reverie in time to hear a creaking on the stair—perhaps that awoke him—and a second later, the jarring door was pushed back on its one creaking hinge. But for the moonlight, the room was dark; and as the door was in shadow, Frank could not make out even the outline of the new-comer. The new-comer looking towards the light, saw a bent figure with a long beard which looked white in the moon-beams. Frank stood to listen, and his profile was thrown out clearly against the light. There was silence for a second, and Penkridge cried, 'Who's there?'

'Have you a candle, Penkridge?' a female voice asked in tones of great sweetness. The owner of the voice looked at the profile from where she stood, and could have borne to look longer, such a picture the clear-cut face and sweeping silver beard and the bent shoulders made. But Frank moved away from

the window, and when Penkridge struck a
light, had thrown himself upon his rough bed
in a shadowed corner, and was shrouded from
observation there.   With a side-glance thrown
towards him swiftly, the new-comer sat down
upon a tea-chest placed for her by Penkridge,
who was imprecating blessings upon her with
a whining fluency.

'I have been to see Mrs. Closky,' she said
when she could get a word in ; and Frank's
eyes, as he regarded her from his shadowed
corner, confirmed his ears, and told him that
she was a lady.   'I am pleased to hear such
an account of you as she gave me.   But why
don't you give up drinking altogether, my
poor fellow ?   I think that if I knew you had
signed the pledge, and would keep it, I could
take you out of this place, and put you into
a situation where you could live in greater
comfort.   Will you try ? '

Mr. Penkridge, who had that evening taken
much more than was good for him, and who
bade fair to go on taking more than was good
for him daily to the end of the chapter, shed
maudlin tears at this appeal.   Which, he said,
he would do anything to oblige such an 'evingly
lady ; but the lady, perceiving his condition,

forebore to press him. 'Is this,' she asked
Penkridge, 'your companion?'

'Yes, ma'am,' replied Penkridge, sobbing
audibly. 'That's the gentleman which I spoke
of, ma'am. And a real good sort he is, ma'am.
Oh yes, ma'am, that he is indeed.'

The visitor turned round, and looked to
where Frank lay upon the heap of shavings
in the corner. 'I know,' she said, 'that you
have been helping me already; and I want
you, if you can, to help me more.'

'In what have I helped you already?' asked
Frank, speaking unwillingly from the darkness.

'I should have said rather that we had
worked together without knowing it.'

'How?' said Frank, helping to keep the
talk going, but much against his inclination.

'There are many in Bolter's Rents who are
very poor and comfortless. I have been trying
to help them a little, but I am almost helpless.
I do not know them; and those who are really
poorest will not let me know them; though
the undeserving come to me with all sorts of
terrible stories. Now, you who know them,
might—'

'I do not know them,' Frank made answer.

'I have tried to meet you before now,' the

visitor continued, 'and finding that you were never at home in the daytime, I came down to-night on purpose to see you. Will you help me?'

'I am as poor as most of those about me,' he answered, and his tone showed more clearly than he intended how little he desired to speak at all.

The visitor persevered. 'You give me the best of all reasons for believing that you will help me. There is no generosity in giving away that which you do not want.'

'I want one thing only, madam,' Frank answered, 'and that I cannot give away.'

'What is that?' the visitor asked quickly.

'My solitude,' he said in answer, and with that he turned his face to the wall.

'I shall try again,' said the visitor, rising to go.

'A second trial can have but one result,' he answered, raising his head, but not turning it. 'It will drive me from the only home I have, and wretched as it is,.I have no wish to leave it.'

'Then,' said the visitor, as she moved towards the door, 'I will trust to time.'

CHAPTER II.

My delirium reached its height in the summer season.

THE first sign of manly down had appeared upon my chin, and since the Crimean War—closed a few years before with great glory if little profit—had left behind it the fashion of beards, I shaved assiduously, to promote the growth of that appanage to manhood. I have above my mantel-piece a portrait of myself taken at that time; and though I know it on good testimony to be accurate, there is in it a flat contradiction of my own remembrances. At eighteen I felt myself quite aged, and I used to look not without pride on incipient wrinkles. In the smooth face which looks upon me from the wall, I find nothing of that stern manhood on which I prided myself. I am not an old man yet, but I am too old to wish for age; though at eighteen I should have been glad to have pitchforked myself into the forties, had such a feat been possible. I wrote a prodigious deal of verse, much of which I remember at this day with an odd mixture of shame and affection. Most of it was addressed to Polly, or in some way concerned her, and she was still my deity.

The time came when I should leave school. I think I feel the emotions proper to that hour more keenly in the remembrance than I did in reality. What a gap it made in life, had I but had the eyes to see it! How many with whom I had spent eight years or part of these in life's journey, faded out of life there and then, and now refuse to be summoned even as the thinnest shadows! It was not of the break in life I left behind, but of the opening to the world which lay before me, that I thought, as the train whirled me homewards. I was not so distinguished in the school as Gascoigne or Gregory had been before me in their last days; but I had done fairly well, and Uncle Ben was amply satisfied. It was not easily possible for Uncle Ben to be balder than he had been in my first

knowledge of him ; but he was greyer than
of old, and his face was more deeply lined.
He was always genial and good-tempered,
and I have known few happier men. His
ambitions were satisfied, even to the gradual
formation of a relationship with the county
magnates ; though he confessed to me privately
that he didn't want them for himself, but only
for the good of the house ; and that if it had
not been for his sons and Maud and me, he
would rather they had continued to stay away.

'But I'll tell you what it is, Johnny,' said
the old man, with a twinkle in his eye. 'It's
the golden bait as draws all them pretty fishes
here. Don't you think now as I overvalue
money. Theer's a lot o' things in the world
as money can't buy, and they're mostly the
things as are best worth havin'. But these
nobs is a poverty-struck lot, and the poor
Major's drove nearly off his head with invita-
tions. Theer ain't a lord in the county as
wouldn't jump at him for a son-in-law. But
then you see I'm a weight to 'em. Theer's no
more polish on me than theer is on so much
oak-bark. I begun too late, Johnny ; and it
ain't no use tryin' to train a tree when it's got
stout and stiff — is it ! Eh ? ' Therewith

Uncle Ben would laugh and poke me in the ribs, and felicitate himself upon the polish which belonged to the Major and to Mr. Horace St. John, the major's brother, and to Maud and me.

The time which came between the last of my school-days and the beginning of my career at college went smoothly, and held only one thing worth chronicling. At that time, a certain police case was reported daily and at length in the London newspapers. An expert in handwriting gave the chief evidence in this case, and there were doubts expressed by some visitor at the breakfast-table as to the value of such testimony as the expert had to offer. The visitor, I remember, was an army man, an old campaigning comrade of the Major's, and he pooh-poohed the whole business.

Uncle Ben broke in calmly. 'Well, I don't know as you can call it a science, but it's a knack. I've had to deal with more than one forgery in my time, sir, and I know a handwriting I've once seen. I don't care how good the disguise is; I can tell it. You may think you've drawn my signature stroke for stroke, and you may practise till you're black in the face if you like, but I'll pick my own out of a hundred; or yours, sir, if the cleverest forger as ever cheated the gallows spent a lifetime in copying it.—No, no, sir! Don't tell me,' said Uncle Ben, who was in some heat by this time. 'There's them as knows what time o' day it is about handwritings.'

'The guv'nah's quite right,' said Major Hartley, 'I've known him do it.'

'Don't you think there's a possibility of being mistaken?' asked the Major's friend.

'Not for a man as has the knack,' Uncle Ben protested stoutly. 'I ain't sticking up for the experts, mind you. They may be duffers and impostors. But the thing is to be done, and *is* done; and there's scores o' men about in business as wouldn't pass the forgery of a name as was known to 'em if they just so much as cast their eye on it.'

'M'm!' said the Major's friend, not yet convinced.

'Well,' said Uncle Ben, 'you get any clever feller to forge anybody's name on me, and see if I don't spot him.' There was a general laugh at this, and the subject dropped. It fell from my mind, until circumstances brought it back again, in a singularly unpleasant manner.

Uncle Ben accompanied me to Oxford and put up at the *Mitre* until he had seen me fairly settled. I took the rooms of a man who had left his furniture and pictures to be sold at a valuation; but all these, at Uncle Ben's instigation, were cleared out, and he furnished me anew. I think he disapproved of the art decorations, which were probably a little too erotic for a quiet taste. When everything was arranged, he came up to the rooms and looked over them with much enjoyment; and finally we sat down together, and he gave me a great deal of advice, drawn from his knowledge of the world. 'I don't think,' he said, 'as you're the sort of feller, Johnny, to be stuck up because you've got a rich uncle; but if *you* don't think of that, there's them as will. Do you remember that feller Tasker coming to my place, three or four years ago?'—I nodded. —'Do you remember what I told you then about bills?'—I nodded again.—'Don't you disappoint me now,' he said with a show of feeling, which was rare in him. 'I sha'n't make you any reg'lar allowance, Johnny; but I shall trust you. Everybody'll know afore you've been here a week as you're the nevey of old Hartley the great millionaire,' — he grinned a little at that,—'and they'll be on to you with offers of unlimited trust and credit. Now, I don't ask you to live stingy; but I ask you to be honest. Don't buy anything you can do without; but at the same time live like a gentleman. If you've got a head on your shoulders, you won't want to buy wine here. I'll send that to you from my own cellars, and you needn't spare it. Write to the butler when you want any. Don't bother me with that; but send me all your bills of whatever sort, and I'll pay 'em. I know what it is when a warm-hearted young chap makes friends, and one of 'em comes to him and says, "I'm in a bit of a hobble, I am. Just put your name on to a bit o' paper for me, will you?" Now this is my last serious word. If you get into a mess yourself, send me word. If you want money — no matter if you're ashamed of what you've come to want it for—send to me. If any one of your friends ever asks you to back his name, you tell him it's more than your income's worth to risk it. For that's the one thing I won't forgive; and now I've told you. If ever you put your name to a bill while I'm alive, I'll disown you. No, no, Johnny. I don't want to threaten you, my lad, and I don't mistrust you ; but you must promise me.'

I gave the promise, and would have thanked him for all his countless kindnesses ; but he stopped me. He gave me a cheque for such an amount that I should have been wasteful indeed had I exceeded it. 'Make it last as long as you can in reason, Johnny,' he said ; and then, with a hearty shake of the hand and a slap on the shoulder, he went down-stairs, blowing his nose so violently that the hollow staircase echoed to the sound.

It is not within my scheme to relate the story of my college life. I fell amongst a wholesome set ; and though I spent more time on the river and in the cricket-ground than I passed above my books, I contrived — considerably to my own surprise — to scratch through for a degree. Uncle Ben was greatly pleased at this, and prophesied that I should make a great man—seeming to regard the achievement of a B.A. degree as a thing till then unheard of. But it is not the life I led in Oxford which comes back to me most strongly when I recall that time. Mr. Fairholt comes within the range of mental vision, for one. I do not think I read him too

unkindly when I believe that he found a wide
difference between the John Campbell who was
cast a friendless orphan on his hands and the
John Campbell who was acknowledged by his
own rich neighbour. I do not think I read
him too unkindly if I say that the money
question made the whole difference. But when
once Uncle Ben had, by sending me to college,
made his responsibility for my future complete,
Mr. Fairholt made me a welcome guest at
Island Hall. In spite of the enormous edifice
Uncle Ben had built, I am fain to confess that
Island Hall remained ' The Hall ' to the
country-people, as it had been time out of
mind before Uncle Ben was heard of. Nor
will I deny that, apart from its one attraction
for me, I liked it better than I liked the
barbaric splendours of my uncle's palace. To
me at that time it was a Bower for Beauty—
nothing more or less. I was welcome there
at all times ; but I took an insane delight in
wandering outside it, and making surreptitious
sketches of it, as though to go near it or to
sketch it had been a thing forbidden. I used
to rise at unearthly hours to ramble there ; and
I used to sketch her window with the Virginia
creeper and the climbing roses about it until I

could have almost drawn them with closed
eyes, until closed eyes can summon them now
at least and see them as clearly as if their
fresh reality were before me. And the dreams
I had! I would go into Parliament, and become Prime Minister, though that went without saying if I once got there. Or I would
go into the army, and distinguish myself in
some tremendous campaign. Or I would go
for authorship—in the poetic line—and write
an epic, and be crowned with bays. But whatever I promised myself—and up to two-and-
twenty one lives in the land of promises, if
not in the Land of Promise—I never ventured
to hope for a happy termination of the pangs
of love. Nobody ever wrote more love-lorn
verses. Nobody was ever more involved in a
more hopeless passion. I used to go about in
the moodiest fashion and watch the sunsets
and the sunrises alone, and improvise verse,
and declaim it in the silent lanes, to the great
astonishment of the yokels, and my own
shamefaced embarrassment when discovered.
I confided my hopeless love to Gascoigne,
who had a curacy hard by; and he used to
smoke his pipe and listen to me with great
forbearance. I confided it to Gregory, who

accepted my belief in my own probable early death with marked composure, and undertook to provide an epitaph. Hawkins of Exeter and Bills of Wadham knew of my helpless and hopeless slavery. I think that in a gloomy way I was rather proud of it. In all the castles I ever built upon this cloud-foundation, there hung no picture of a happy union. I was going to be great, and then I was going to die ; and Polly was to know how splendid a treasure she had cast aside. Yet I cannot remember that she treated me with anything but kindness, and I know she must have had a difficult task at times.

My delirium reached its height in the summer season which followed the close of my time at college. Polly had a paid com- panion, and Miss Hurd and I were great in friendship. I suppose Miss Hurd was thirty if she were a day ; but we were kindred spirits, spite of this disparity of years. She had a fine deep melancholy-sounding contralto, and she used to sing, in what I took to be a patent allusion to my own case,—

> ' Let us talk of love no more
> While the bat is flying ;
> Fitter friendship's solemn lore
> When the day is dying.'

Other ditties bearing on her own condition
she sang, as though the lower octaves of an
organ were concealed within her.   She could
not sing the old songs, and the like.   Except
for a general and uncultivated fondness for
the art, I was not in any manner musical ; but
I used to shake my head at this, and murmur
inly that *I* could not sing the old songs either
—a question as to which there existed no
shadow of a doubt.   I supposed that Miss
Hurd was aware of my passion, until one
evening when I came across the fields on
horseback and found Polly absent.   Miss
Hurd sat at the piano and played ' The Heart
Bowed Down,' and I, sitting at the window,
sighed as I thought of my own.

' You are not well, Mr. Campbell,' said Miss
Hurd.

There was a dusky light in the room, and
the window was open, and the quiet scents
and gently stealing sounds of the country
mingled with it soothingly.   I rose and
crossed to the piano, and said with much
solemnity that I was well enough—' In body,'
I added with a sigh.

' Thou canst not minister,' said Miss Hurd in
her lowest contralto tones, ' to a mind diseased.'

'No,' I answered, sighing again, and carried on the quotation, though when I reached the 'yesterday,' I thought it a little inappropriate.

'What is it, Mr. Campbell?' said Miss Hurd. 'Confide in me.'

I seized Miss Hurd's passive hand as it lay upon the keys of the pianoforte, and I, told her in sepulchral tones that my heart was breaking. I believe I quite believed it.

'With what?' asked Miss Hurd. But I returned no answer. She pressed my hand, and murmured again, 'With what, Mr. Campbell? Confide in me.'

'With love!' I answered, not unconscious of a comic side to the whole episode, the mere hint of which in my own mind made me perhaps a trifle more morose and tragic than before.

'For whom?' said Miss Hurd with my hand in both of hers. I laid my melancholy head upon the cold smooth polish of the top of the piano, and murmured my divinity's name. Miss Hurd dropped my hand, and sat still in the dusk of the room and made no sign. How she left the room, I know not. Nor do I know how *I* left it; but when I came to myself, I was in the fields again in the moonlight, putting Bob at a fence. I screeched with demoniac laughter. Miss Hurd! In love with Miss Hurd! Could she have dreamed of it? Could Polly have thought it? Horror! And I laughed bitterly to myself as I said that this was Fate's last and cruellest burden, and I would endure no more.

I resolved that I would go over next day, and compel Polly to turn spiritual dentist; but when morning came, the thought of Miss Hurd daunted me; and I hung about the stables in a weak irresolute way, until to my self-worrying mind, the very stable-helpers could read my vacillation and its cause; and I rode away in self-defence. Miss Hurd daunted me, as I have said; but though she held me back from the house with the memory of last night's episode, she could not keep me, nor could I keep myself, away from its neighbourhood. And there, as those serio-comic Fates who rule the destinies of lovers would have it, I found Polly alone in the fresh green lanes, with a frond of fern in her little gauntleted hand, and a wreath of young oak-leaves twined about her hat. I dismounted, and walked by her side, in a

foolish compound mood of ecstasy and misery.
Prompted by those serio-comic Destinies, I
must needs drift in mystic and bewildering
speech about last evening's episode with Miss
Hurd. I tried at first to assume a tone
of banter, which failed me miserably. Had
Polly, so I asked her, ever deigned in her
own mind to associate me with the matri-
monial condition? Had she ever contemplated the possibility or probability of my
being some day married? She regarded me
gravely and frankly, but without a suspicion
of humour or confusion. No, she said; she
had never thought of me in that connection.

'But,' she added, standing still to speak,
and shading her eyes with the fern, held
lightly in both hands, and making the sweet-
est picture with beautiful unconsciousness,
'you are getting to be a man, Jack. And
I suppose,' with her eyes opening just a
thought wider at the fancy, 'that I'm getting to be a woman. One is a woman at
eighteen, I think. Do you know'—she spoke
as though this were altogether a discovery—
'I think that a girl is more a woman at
eighteen, than a boy is a man at twenty.'

In my bewildered compound mood, this hurt my feelings. It seemed to widen the space between us, and to make despair more despairing. Canon Kingsley's charming novel of *Two Years Ago* was new just then ; and I asked Polly, who had read it recently, if she remembered a passage in which it is declared—apropos of a Mr. Creed, who carried a warlike message to Tom Thurnall— that if a man is ever to be a man he will be one at twenty.

'Oh yes,' said Polly, holding to her colours ; 'but I think a woman is more a woman at eighteen.'

But, I persisted, with an aching feeling that my head was growing empty—had she ever thought that I was in love ? With—with— anybody ?

'No,' she answered, facing round again, with the fern still lightly balanced in both hands above her eyes. I felt that I had a hangdog guilty look, and beneath her glance I could feel that unpleasant aspect deepen. A little light of humour in her eyes ripened into a full smile of friendly mirth. 'O Jack,' she said, 'is this a confession ?' Before I could answer or think of answering, her sudden question had so staggered and bewildered me, she dropped the fern, and clapped her hands together. 'It is Miss Hurd!' she said with a gravity as sudden as the gesture; and with the swift vivacity which was a part of her, and is still, she passed her arm through mine, and in a tone of cosy confidential friendship, she said, 'Tell me all about it.'

'O Polly,' I cried, not thinking how answerable I was for the situation, 'how could you think such a thing of me?'

'I don't know,' said Polly, with a little shrug. 'Miss Hurd is very nice, I'm sure.'

'I daresay,' I answered with Byronic bitterness of soul.

'I beg your pardon, I am sure,' said Polly, moving her arm a little to-and-fro in mine, as if to decide upon the most comfortable position there. 'And now,' she said, giving my arm a little hug, as if to emphasize her own satisfaction in the approaching confidence, 'tell me all about it.'

I said, 'Never mind,' darkly; and Polly said coaxingly, 'Yes; now do tell me all about it.'

I responded still darkly that she would know some day; and at that she was a little offended, and withdrew her arm. The empty aching of my head left me incapable of doing or saying anything to retrieve myself; but it left me the power to make myself feel still more hangdog and more desperate. Perhaps, I said, she did not care to know. It could make no difference to her.

'How can you say so?' she demanded with a little flash of her old childish petulance. Then with stately gravity, 'You are a stupid boy. You are undecided and self-contradictory, and'—with a complete change of face and voice, she took my arm again—'I am sure that you are not happy; and if I can help you, you must let me do it.'

I was quite melted at this, and told her that I felt I was a villain; but I added that it had been my fate all my lifetime to appear before her in an unfavourable aspect.

'That is all vanity,' she said, with calm decisiveness. 'You have always been a little too self-conscious. Fight against it.'

'No,' I said, desperately, 'I have been awkward and constrained before you all my life.'

'Before me?' she asked in a voice which told me she was wounded.

'Yes,' I answered; 'and before you only. Ever since I saw you first, when Aunt Bertha took me to the nursery, and introduced me to you as your cousin.'

I had thought she would know my meaning; but her tone convinced me that she was still ignorant of it. She answered only, 'You are very unkind and cross to-day.'

'Unkind to myself,' I responded fatuously; 'but not so unkind as I deserve.'

'You are incomprehensible,' she answered in a tone of pique; and we walked on in silence until we came to the gate of the drive, when she asked me smilingly if I would 'Come in and be good.' Baffled in my purpose, and being altogether wretched and forlorn, I shook my head, and gave her my hand in silence.

'Bring your Œdipus with you,' said Polly lightly, 'if you come again in so Sphinx-like a humour.'

'I will send him by the penny-post,' I answered, conscious of a lucid interval and a resolve.

'He shall be welcome,' said Polly with a laugh; and then with a nod and a bright 'Good-day' she passed out of sight behind the curve of the trees.

I mounted Bob again, and in the tumult of
my feelings, took him helter-skelter over the
fields homeward. Arrived, I sought the solitude of my chamber, and sat down to abuse
myself for being so egregious an ass. I had
said nothing I meant to say, and had said
many things I had no right to say. I remembered my share in the whole conversation, and
blushed over its inconsequence, its testiness, its
want of purpose. I caught sight of my own
face in the glass, and shook my head at myself
savagely, announcing with perfect seriousness
that if I could only get outside myself, I would
kick myself from there to Land's End for an
impracticable, disgraceful, unworthy idiot ! I
tried to write a letter to Polly, and made thirty
or forty beginnings, and threw them all aside.
So far as they went, I believe they all breathed
unalterable devotion and a desire to die. I
began one, I can remember, with, ' What am
I, O pure and beautiful, that I should dare— ; '
' Dear　Polly' 　sounded　too 　familiar ; 　and
' Dearest Miss Fairholt '—apart from the distant
coldness of the form—seemed to suggest that
there were several Misses Fairholt—three at
least. Why then, I thought, should I use any
introductory phrase at all ? Why not plunge

in medias res, like 'some epic poets?' Whilst
I sat thus bewildered, a message came from
Uncle Ben, who desired to see me; and having
crammed the blotted and crumpled pile of
unfinished notes into an escritoire and locked
them there, I obeyed the summons.

Uncle Ben was strolling in the gardens,
smoking a big porcelain German pipe. 'Have
you got any notions, young un, about your
future?' was the question with which he met
me. I had within five minutes expressed the
ideas I had upon that point in writing; but
feeling that Uncle Ben would scarcely care
to know that I meditated an early death, and
was quite indifferent as to what came before
it, I contented myself by asking if *he* had
thought about anything for me.

'I've thought about 'em all,' said Uncle
Ben. 'Theer's the church, and theer's law,
and theer's physic, and theer's th' army and
navy. One, two, three, four, five. Then
theer's art, and theer's litterychewer. I take
it for granted as you ain't got a special call
to neither of them two.'—I believed I had to
each of them, but I kept silence.—'Well then,
about the church?' he questioned, turning
round upon me with a finger on a thumb in

act to tell off the five.—I shook my head,
having very serious and decided ideas on that
matter.—'Very well. About the law? How
should you like to be a barrister?'—I had
but a mean idea of the legal profession, and
I said so.—'Very well,' said my uncle, going
on to the middle finger. 'Then theer's physic.
Now, th' army and navy is only professions
to them that's got a lot o' money, and don't
want a profession. To anybody else they're
slavery. How about physic?'

I thought I saw that 'physic' was what
Uncle Ben most favoured, and I said 'Yes'
tentatively.

' It's a honourable profession,' said my uncle,
' and it's a useful un. Now, what do you say
to physic?'

I told him I thought I would say 'Yes' to
physic; and he asked me then what I should
say to Dr. Brand.

' A really first-rate man, Johnny,' said Uncle
Ben. 'Last time I was in town, I asked him
if in a few years' time he'd be prepared to
admit a smart feller into his place to look
around him; and we had a bit of a talk about
it; and he's willing to take you under his
wing, my lad; and make a friend of you, and

make a man of you. You'll see if you like
it; and if you don't, you needn't stick to it.
It's a great favour, mind you; but he'll look
after you when you get up there, and you
must cultivate him.'

It seemed all very easily settled; and Uncle
Ben, who was always for striking whilst the
iron was hot, advised me to go at once to
London and spend a week there—see Dr.
Brand—walk through the hospitals, get a first
general idea of things, and decide as soon as
I could see my way to a decision.

'Look here,' said Uncle Ben, clapping me
jovially on the shoulder, 'we'll go up to-
morrer, and have a look round together. Eh,
Johnny?'

That was settled at once. I made a fire
of the blotted and crumpled fragments of
notes, and sent a brief letter to Polly. Uncle
Ben's proposal had cleared my wits a little, I
suppose; for I wrote without overwhelming
embarrassment that Œdipus and I were going
up to town with Mr. Hartley, that we all
three hoped to be improved by the trip,
and that it was probable that the journey
would result in my adoption of a profession.
And having despatched this letter, I lay for

a long time awake, a little excited by the prospect of life in London, and a good deal less disposed to an early death on desert shores. When I fell asleep, I dreamed that I was appointed Physician in Ordinary to the Queen, and that I was Sir John Campbell.

CHAPTER III.

HISTORY.

*He could not guess that the lost friend had been so near
to him.*

DR. BRAND was driving down Piccadilly,
or rather was being carried along that
thoroughfare, one blazing, glaring, dusty summer afternoon. He sat rounding his shoulders,
with his elbows on his knees and his chin on
his hands, looking straight before him and
seeing nothing. The open carriage in which
he rode and the pair of bays which drew it,
were among the best of their kind; for Dr.
Brand was prospering greatly, and had a taste
in equipages and horse-flesh, which he could
afford to gratify. The turn-out was remarkably
unprofessional, as might be expected in the
case of a man so little conventional in all
things. The doctor was so deeply absorbed

in the endeavour to solve the matter in his mind, that he did not notice a figure on horseback which came between him and the sunlight. The figure was that of a soldierly-looking bronzed young fellow who had lost an arm. The light-brown beard, with something of a reddish tinge in it, and the close military cut of the hair, together with a certain set solidity of figure which had not of old belonged to him, might have made it necessary even for an old friend to look twice before he recognised Arthur Hastings. There was the same calm look of lazy and impudent humour in his eyes, though his bronzed skin made them seem curiously light in colour; and though his ancient jauntiness of carriage was subdued, it showed itself a little still. He rode on alongside, until the doctor became aware of the figure between him and the sunlight, and gave it a cursory glance of no-recognition.

'Why,' said a voice, 'should Æsculapius drive like Jehu, son of Nimshi?'

The doctor turning, rose in his carriage and held out a hand of cordial welcome.

Hastings shook his head, and nodded in the direction of his empty sleeve. 'Can't,' he said.

'If I loosed the beggar,'—indicating his horse
by another nod,—'he'd bolt.   How d'ye do?'

The doctor called to the coachman to bring
the horses to a walk; and Hastings having
subdued his horse's inclination to get into the
carriage, went soberly alongside.

'When did you get back?' asked the doctor.

'Day before yesterday,' said Hastings.   'Was
just coming round when I saw you.'

'I never heard of *that*, said the doctor
bluntly, nodding at the empty sleeve.   'When
did you get it?'

'I got it,' said Hastings, 'if you mean the
limb, very early in life indeed, and parted with
it about three days after the last racket at the
Malakoff.'

'Never heard of it,' said the doctor; 'though
I heard you did your duty there, sir.'

'Thank you,' said Hastings, simply and sincerely.   Early in their knowledge of each
other, the elder man had given a little lecture
to the other, in which he had developed his own
ideas of duty with almost brutal plainness.

'Where do you come from now?' the doctor
asked.

'From roaming to and fro in the earth, and
going up and down in it.'

'Doing something better, I hope,' said the doctor, 'than quote Satan by the way?'

'Better at times, I think.—Are you busy?'

'I am always busy.   Nobody has a right to be anything else.'

'Some men are born idle,' said Hastings; 'some achieve idleness; and some have idleness thrust upon them.'

'Will you dine with me to-night?' asked the doctor. 'Eight o'clock. Don't dress. I never dress for dinner. Absurd habit. Won't encourage it at my table. Will you come?'

'On wings swift as meditation or the thoughts of love,' responded Hastings; and the doctor, waving his hand, cried 'Good-bye' and 'Drive on' in a breath, and was gone in a cloud of dust of his own raising. With a parting nod, the young man turned back and rode up the blazing street, passing a dusky Smyrniote, who in the uniform of an English groom had followed him at orthodox distance, and now resumed his place, and came on soberly in true oriental indifference to the glances levelled at him by the curious. When Hastings reached the doctor's house, a little before the appointed time, the Smyrniote accompanied him still, and took up his stand

in the hall outside the dining-room door, where
he startled Mrs. Brand more than a little, as
she passed him on her way upstairs from an
inspection of the kitchen. She made no remark about him, however; but the doctor
coming in a moment later with Major Hartley
in his train, had no scruple of delicacy.

'Where did you pick up the nigger?' he
asked.

'I picked up the nigger,' Hastings returned
—'to copy your own ungraceful locution—on
the tented field.'

'Why do you carry him about in England?'
asked the doctor ungraciously.

'Well, you see,' said Hastings, with a little
flush upon his face, which nobody remarked,
'he took to carrying *me* about at first.'

'Now, that's not fayah, Hastings,' said Major
Hartley, twirling his big moustaches with both
hands.—'That's quaite unfayah, Mrs. Brand,
I ashaw yaw.' The longer the Major lived,
the more he drawled, and the wilder grew his
dandified distortions of his native tongue.
The doctor and his wife looked at Hastings,
who blushed palpably, and had nerve enough
to utter no more than 'Pooh!' The confusion of so fluent a person was too remark-

able to go unnoticed, and both looked inquiringly at the Major. 'What an extwordinary fellah you are, Hastings, to be shaw!' said the Major.—'Now you'd really think, Mrs. Brand, that a fellah would be proud of a thing like that.'

'Of a thing like what?' asked Mrs. Brand.

'Don't be an ass, Hartley,' said Hastings in a low, rapid tone, which was not intended for anybody but the Major, but was heard clearly by all three. The Major laughed pleasantly, with a look of mischief; and Hastings walked to the window with an abrupt and angry step.

'I insist on relating the incident,' said the Major; 'but in consideration of yaw feelings, I'll be brief. Hastings fetched the niggah out of a regulah storm of fiah one day, when the poor beggah was wounded by a fragment of a shell. Three months latah the nigger retaliated, and fetched Hastings out of a storm of fiah, when he was lying quite helpless with a broken arm. And since then, they've been inseparables; and bay Jove! Mrs. Brand, I think they ought to be. Don't you, madam, now, don't you?'

The doctor strode across the room, and brought his hand down heavily on Hastings' shoulder with a loud cry of 'Bravo!' 'And

said the doctor, facing round with an air of
serio-comedy, ' I'll knock the next man down,
or woman either, who dares to say a word
about it.'

An hour had passed, and dinner was nearly
over before Hastings had recovered his equani-
mity ; and for the first time in any man's knowledge of him, he was depressed at a scene
which should have been festive. When the
doctor found him gradually recovering from
the effects of the Major's exposure, he renewed
his inquiries as to the movements Hastings had
made since the close of the war.

' I come last,' he answered, 'from Basuto
Land. I went from Hong-kong to Ceylon,
and found a man with a steam-yacht who
wanted to go to the Cape of Good Hope, and
could get nobody to chum with him. So we
cast in our lot together ; but I found him can-
tankerously inclined, and left him at the Cape,
and rambled about alone.

' What took you to Hong-kong ?' asked
the doctor.

' Well,' said Hastings,' ' I had some notions
about going into the House at that time ; and
since a man must have a crotchet there of
one sort or another, I thought the opium-

trade would serve for mine, and went out there to look at it.'

'What made you change you mind?'

'I don't think I did change my mind,' he answered with a flippancy which was more a thing of habit than of feeling. 'I think my mind changed me. Anyhow, I came to the belief that there were things better worth doing than going into the House.'

'Ah!' said the doctor. 'What are they?'

'I'll tell you one of them some of these days,' said Hastings calmly.

'By the way,' asked Dr. Brand, 'do you remember Bolter's Rents?'

'Bolter? Bolter?' said Hastings questioningly. 'I had a horse of that name once, and he deserved it.' Then with perfect irrelevance, he quoted, 'For the blood-boltered Banquo smiles on me.'

'Bolter's Rents,' said the doctor, 'is a haunt of thieves, and worse—a haunt of cadgers, tramps, crossing-sweepers, the riff-raff of the London streets; a tumble-down fever-den; a brick-and-mortar ulcer.

'Ah! yes,' said Hastings; 'I remember. A place off Oxford Street. Mrs. Brand was interested in some people there.'

' It's in the market,' said the doctor.

' If I knew the owner,' said Hastings, with an approach to a smile, ' I might recommend him to somebody who would draw up a description of the place, and help him to sell it to some advantage.'

' I want to help him to sell it,' said the doctor. ' But can we talk about that matter at another time.'

The talk drifted into other channels ; and a little later than ten o'clock the Major took his leave, pleading an engagement at the Opera, which he had so far deserted for the pleasure of meeting Hastings.

' Now,' said the doctor, settling himself easily in a deep arm-chair, ' light another cigar, fill your glass, and settle down to talk. I want you to do justice to yourself. You have heart and brains, and you mustn't waste them. Have you found a purpose yet ? '

' Two or three,' said Hastings.

' I want to give you another,' said the doctor, ' if your hands are not too full. That place I spoke of—Bolter's Rents—is one of the disgraces of London. If it got into the hands of a good man, it might be made a credit to any city. If it gets into the hands of an ordinary speculator, it will be pulled down, and its inhabitants will go all adrift into other places of its kind. If it came into the possession of a man who considered those poor wretches, it might be gradually rebuilt, and altogether purified, physically and morally. The poverty might live there still under cleanly conditions, and the scoundrelism be hunted out of it, or taught to behave itself; and the thing—though it could not yield an extraordinary profit—could be made to pay. I sha'n't apologise for suggesting this to you; for I believe it's just the sort of thing you want.'

'Don't you think the better course would be to pull the place down at once and build anew?' asked Hastings.

'No,' said the doctor. 'There are a hundred people there who are half-civilised already, who would be scattered to the four winds in that way. If the place could be mended gradually, we could keep them together, and they would help under better circumstances to leaven the mass about them.'

'I will look into the matter,' said Hastings, 'and let you know what I think of it. Where is the place?'

The doctor described it. An entry between
two shops, numbered so-and-so, led to a court.
There was no mistaking it. The name of the
agent who had the sale of the property was
noted ; and shortly before midnight, Hastings
took his leave with the faithful Smyrniote behind him. The doctor's proposal went exactly
with his own desires ; and if the truth had
been known, I am inclined to believe that it
was chiefly with the idea of saving money for
some such coup as this that Hastings had
spent so much of his time in travel. Wish-
ing to see the place at once, he turned into
Oxford Street, and walked leisurely towards
Bolter's Rents. The moon rode in a sky
which was almost cloudless, and the street
gleamed before him like a river. He reached
the entrance to the court, and looked down
its black perspective to the one dull lamp
which twinkled at the bottom. 'Gel bourda,
Ali,' said he to his servant ; and the man
came, and followed him closely down the fetid
way, where nameless odours reminded him
of the popular bath of his native land. They
marched once or twice round the court-
yard, Hastings looking up at the disreputable
buildings, and the man following him in

wonder. A door near at hand grated on the
gritty floor of one of the ground-rooms, and
a bearded man came out into the court with
a basin, which he emptied upon the broken
pavement. He looked up at Hastings and
his servant and passed by, leaving the door
through which he had passed still open. The
light of a candle shone through the doorway;
and Hastings glancing in, saw a man tossing
miserably on the quarried floor, upon a couch
of straw and sacking. He had heard the
murmur of a voice on passing the door in
his first slow journey round the court, and
knew it now for this sick man's moaning.
Beckoning Ali to follow, he entered the room
and looked about him; and it is not too
much to say that he shook and sickened with
pity and loathing. The man who lay upon
the floor was muttering rapidly to himself in
German, and tossing a weary head from side
to side. Since we saw Hastings last, he had
seen much of the world, and had looked on
many of its worst troubles. But he had never
dreamed of anything like the horror of this
place being possible in England. I can only
tell you of its desolation—not of its filth, for
to set that down would be to make myself

unreadable. The man himself, with his vast beard of matted black swaying to and fro across his half-naked chest, and his wild hair nearly a foot long straggling down to meet it, was terrible to look at. His eyes and his teeth gleamed as he rocked his head from side to side, and he moaned ever and always of trifles probably forgotten until fever brought a stimulant to memory before quenching it. Hastings, who spoke German better than most Englishmen, addressed the man in his own tongue, asking if he could be of use to him ; but he received no answer, and stood sorrowfully helpless for the minute, until the man he had first seen returned with the basin balanced carefully in both hands. The new-comer called out in German in some cheering phrase as he entered, and did not at first observe the two intruders. He started a little when he saw them, but said nothing, and kneeling down, busied himself by administering to his patient the contents of the basin.

' Has this man been long in this condition ? ' Hastings asked in English.

The man still tended the other, and returned no answer, but started again visibly at the sound of the voice. Hastings put his question into German.

'Yes,' the nurse answered in the same tongue, with his voice muffled in his grey beard and his head bent above his patient.

'Is he a friend of yours?'

'No.'

'Do you live here?'

The man pointed upwards to the roof, but gave no other answer. Hastings stood silent for a moment, and then asked, 'Has the man no other nurse?'

'No,' was the answer, still muffled by the beard.

'Can you not remove him to an hospital?'

'He will go to-morrow,' the man responded, assiduously bending over his patient.

Hastings' accustomed ear caught the sound of an accent foreign to the language in which the man spoke. 'You are not a German,' he said. 'What are you?'

No answer was returned; and Hastings, thinking that the fellow's nationality was no business of his if he chose to conceal it, stood for a little while and watched the feeding of the patient. By-and-by he asked what the sick man was suffering from.

' Fever,' said the nurse briefly.

' Is the disease contagious ? '

' Yes.'

' Are you not afraid of catching it ? '

' No.'

' How long have you tended the man ? '

' To-night only.'

' Has any one else attended him ? '

' No.'

' If I give you a little money, will you expend it on him, and send him comfortably to the hospital ? '

' I have given notice, and he will be sent for to-morrow.'

' Then you do not want money ? '

' No.'

' How do you live ? '

' I work.'

' At what ? '—No answer.—' Is there much sickness here ? Are you often employed in this way ? '

' Sometimes.'

' Who summoned you here to take care of this man ? Who told you he was ill ? '

' Nobody.'

Hastings crossed over to the patient, who lay quieter now ; and the nurse walked away

and looked out through the open door.
Ali stood by, and marvelled, but said
nothing. He had implicit confidence in his
master, and believed that all he did was right.
'What is there in that face I know?' his
master was thinking to himself as he bent
above the fever-stricken wretch on the floor.
'Is it a fancy? Have I seen the face in the
street? Whose is it?' He could find no
answer in his thoughts, though he called scores
of faces to remembrance. 'I have seen this
man somewhere before,' he said aloud. 'Do
you know who he is?' He received no
answer; and turning round, he saw that the
nurse had disappeared. After standing irresolute for a moment, he left the place and walked
back into Oxford Street, where he went on
until he saw the red lamp of a surgeon,
whom he summoned. The medical man did
not care to enter Bolter's Rents at that time
of night without a policeman, and indeed
flatly refused to do so; but an officer was
soon found, and he, happy in the douceur
Hastings gave, led the way with an air of
protection.

'I cannot help thinking,' said Hastings to
the surgeon, as the latter knelt down to feel

the patient's wrist, 'that I have seen the man before somewhere.'

The patient was murmuring still in German ; but when Hastings spoke thus, he paused and seemed to listen. When he began again, he spake in nasal English, and Hastings fancied he heard his own name amidst the murmurings. Stooping lower, he heard distinctly. It was of no use, the man was saying ; he really couldn't do it. Money was very tight jhoost now.

'Tasker ?' cried the listener suddenly, in a voice of amazement. The sick man made a motion to rise, but fell back again. For a moment, at the cry, his eyes took an aspect of intelligence ; but the unearthly brightness of fever returned, and Tasker—for it was he —went back to his German murmurings.

'This man was a money-lender in the City six or seven years ago,' said Hastings, in answer to the look of astonishment and inquiry with which the surgeon regarded him. 'I had dealings with him in my nonage. He was almost scoundrel enough to deserve even this ; but I was amazed to find him here. Where is the man who was tending him ?'

The bearded man was just outside the door,

and had heard the talk and the cry of recognition. Hastings stepping to the door,
called after him as he drew off in the shadow
of the great overhanging wall. The policeman
who was posturing at the door with a set of
knuckles at his ribs in the region of his waist-
belt, inquired if his honour wanted that man.
Hastings, scarcely knowing why, said 'Yes ;'
and the policeman went after him and brought
him back. He came submissively with downcast looks.

'Why do you want me ?' he asked in
German. 'Let me go. I trouble nobody.'

'Take that,' said Hastings with a sudden
impulse, slipping a sovereign into the hand
which waved towards him in appeal. 'Good-
night.'

With bent head he drew back into the
shadow, and the deeper shade of the doorway
seemed to absorb him as he entered it.

'Curious characrter that, sir,' said the officer,
stiffly posturing like a model for a comic
sculptor. 'Quite the gentleman to speak to.
Name of Jones. Had a quarter of a millying
o' money, and lost it all on three Derbies.
Calls him the Dook round about here and at
the Docks where he works.'

' Indeed ! ' said Hastings, beginning to wonder whether all the residents of Bolter's Rents
were broken men of substance. ' Have you
known him long ? '

' Hever since he come to grief, sir. I
was at the Heast-end of the town for several
'ears, and knowed him at the Docks, Quiet,
hinnerffensive feller, sir, as ever lived.'

Why was it, Hastings asked himself, as
he walked to his hotel, with Ali in his place
behind him, that the image of a dead friend
who fell before Sebastopol should be so closely
with him ? An echo of Frank Fairholt's
voice was in his ear ; in his mind's eye he saw
the friendly, candid eyes and the handsome
wilful face, and in his heart he repented of
the evil of his youth, and his spirit was sorely
troubled.

' It was my fault mainly,' he confessed, ' that
poor Frank went wrong at all. But time is
merciful ; and most of the griefs his loss
created have been healed. And he is at rest,
poor Frank, at least.' He saw the little round
of palisades which marked the spot behind
the trenches where the dead soldier lay, and
the black knolls here and there which covered
his old comrades. He could not guess—how

should he ?—that the lost friend had been so near to him.   How could he dream that Frank Fairholt was kneeling lonely in that dark fever-den, praying God for patience that he might bear his burden to the end !

CHAPTER IV.

AUTOBIOGRAPHY.

*' Tell me what you believe against me, and I will
clear myself.'*

I WENT up to town next day with Uncle
Ben, according to arrangement. I found
Dr. Brand a trifle brusque and dictatorial, I
thought; but learning that years must elapse
before he would undertake to do more than
take a friendly interest in me, I thought I
should manage to get along with him very
nicely. In the great school of medicine and
surgery in which I presently found myself a
pupil, Dr. Brand was regarded with profound
respect. One of the first things pointed out
to me in the hospital museum was a dissec-
tion of the human arm, in which every nerve
and vein and artery and muscle was displayed
in most delicate and exquisite network. That

was Dr. Brand's doing; and it was looked on as something next to a miracle of dexterity and art. I saw him in the operating theatre, where he stood almost unrivalled. At first, his perfect calm, the insouciance with which he went to the most terrible performances, shocked and disgusted me, and I thought him a monster of no-feeling. But in a week or two, I began to be better able to understand and value his quiet mastery; and in a month he was my special hero.

It has been a problem to many, how it comes about that the orderly and gentlemanly men who make up the rank-and-file of medicine and surgery in these islands are evolved from the disorderly and rowdy youth who make up the staple of our medical-student supply. I confess myself the more unable to solve this problem because I have been intimate with the embryonic and with the complete surgeon, and have known and noted the marvellous space which severs them. In Oxford, I had known reading sets, and boating sets, and drinking and gambling sets, and sets of all sorts. But though I found men here given over to the same variety of pursuits, they went about them for the most part in so different a manner, and were themselves of so different an order, that I seemed to be thrown into quite an unfamiliar life among them. I had been so accustomed to the control of money, that town-life offered me no new temptations to extravagance. Of all the keen things Balzac has written, there is none keener than that passage in which he declares of an extravagant woman that she was reckless in the profligacy of her waste *because* she had known a time when a sou's worth of fried potatoes would have been a luxury to her. But it never occurred to me to do less than spend what Uncle Ben allowed me, and I found my society sought by some for whom I had little affection. How it fared with Uncle Ben's sons, my cousins, I can only conjecture; but I know that my relationship to the great millionaire was converted into one of the miseries of my life, by the adulation it secured me, and the prominence it occasionally gave me. Mr. Wickamby, senior demonstrator, was marvellously fond of me, and undertook to introduce me to scientific society in London. I went to an assemblage of ladies and gentlemen in his company at one time, and was finding an innocent interest in the display of divers new inventions, when a whisper from Wickamby—'The nephew of Hartley —Hartley Hall, you know—the great millionaire'—came in upon my quiet, and my night was spoiled. There was a gilt pasteboard erection of cubic form at one end of the room, which was supposed to represent the exact amount of gold in circulation in the British Islands; and whilst I regarded this, and thought how small a sum of money it represented per head for the population, Mr. Wickamby came up and laughed, and said in the voice of a public lecturer, that my uncle, Mr. Hartley of Hartley Hall, could show a considerable slice of that if he desired to—eh? Ha! ha! The baleful whisper followed me into remote corners, 'Nephew of Hartley. Great millionaire, Hartley. Quite a self-made man.'

There was a doctor of divinity there who was most ponderously polite to me, and who took the keenest interest in my uncle and my welfare. He delivered a little oration to me on the dangers and advantages of wealth; and whenever anybody passed the corner in which he had me penned, he would inter-

rupt the current of his speech to summon
the passer-by, and would ask to be per-
mitted to introduce Mr. Campbell, 'nephew
of Mr. Hartley, the distinguished millionaire.'
The coarse greed with which I found myself
surrounded, not for money, but for leave to
talk about it, would have been matter for
laughter, if I had not been the centre of it.
As it was, however, it became unbearable, and
I withdrew myself stealthily.

I had rooms in Clement's Inn, light airy
chambers, looking out upon upon a square of
green, bordered by fine trees. The rooms look
now upon the New Law Courts, which have
been so long a-building, and the grass is still
there before them, and the trees yet flourish.
I was mightily proud of those chambers at
the first, and was perhaps as happy in them
as I have ever been elsewhere. 'What more
felicitie,' asks the poet, 'can fall to creature?
Than to enjoye delighte with libertie?' Mr.
Wickamby, the senior demonstrator, would
sometimes visit me of an afternoon and take
a glass of Burgundy and a cigar. He was a
man who smiled, a comfortable man, with a
saponaceous manner. He had little set forms
of speech for all manner of circumstances

and contingencies, which he used by rote, as though they were formulæ out of the Pharmacopœia. One of these was that it really seemed absurd to say it, but if ever at any moment I found myself in want of funds, I was to apply to him, and consider him my banker. It was so easy, he would add, to run out of coin in town. At first, it crossed me that this was the prelude to a request for a loan; but Mr. Wickamby never tried my regard in that way; and he used to utter his formula so heartily, that I grew positively grateful to him for his benevolence.

But there were pleasanter visitors than Mr. Wickamby at my chambers in Clement's Inn, and amongst the pleasantest were Gascoigne and Æsop. Gascoigne's clerical duties held him hard and fast in the country all the year, with the exception of one fortnight, which he spent with me. I met him at the railway station, and brought him home in great glee, and enthroned him in an arm-chair.

'What prospects?' I asked him. 'When are you going to be a bishop?'

'I don't know,' he answered laughingly. But he added more gravely, and as I thought with a touch of regretfulness, 'I ought to have stayed on at college, Jack, and taken a fellowship. But I should never have had the living which is to be mine unless I had put my neck into the yoke of this curacy. The patron insists on having a working man, and I am working. One of the ameliorations,' he said, laughing again, 'is that they don't consider cricket wicked in our part of the world.'

I said somewhat hotly at this, that the servants of the Church were surrounded by foolish restrictions, and that none seemed more absurd to me than the denial of harmless outdoor sports. I could see a reason, perhaps, against hunting; but there were a dozen other things which I enumerated in which, as I believed, there lay harm neither for a clergyman nor for his flock.

'You are wrong, Jack,' said Gascoigne seriously. 'But the drawback in the Church of England is that the influence secured is not commensurate with the sacrifice ordained. The true sacerdotal power is not wielded by any man in our Church, even though he may make all the concessions which should secure it. The power of the Church at large is great; but the openings to indi-

vidual ambition are few. There is an open
avenue to fame and power in the Church of
Rome ; and though you may not think it,
there is a way as broad and certain among
the great schismatic sects — Congregational
and Wesleyan. Amongst *us*, the individual
withers, and the Church is more and more.
Spurgeon is more of a personality than even
the Archbishop of Canterbury.'

'Then,' I asked, ' you are not satisfied ? '

'"Which of us,"' he quoted, ' " *is* satisfied
in this world ? Which of us has his desire ? "'

'But,' I urged, 'there is surely some joy in
fighting a good cause, even as one of the rank-
and-file ? '

'Ay,' said Gascoigne ; 'surely. But there
would be more joy perhaps in leading the
combatants.'

'In what direction ? ' I asked him.

He laughed, and threw his hands abroad
with a careless gesture. 'Perhaps one might
see,' he answered, 'a little farther on horseback.'

I loved him so sincerely and admired him
so much, that this seeming flippancy grieved
me, and I let the subject go. 'Æsop will
be here directly,' I told him. 'I have asked

him especially to come this evening; but I have not told him that you will be here. I kept that for a surprise.'

There was a little constraint upon me as I said this; for I did not wish it to appear that I dissented seriously from any mood of his. Lest he should observe this, I arose as I spoke, and seizing one of his portmanteaus, dragged it into his bedroom. It was a little surprising that he returned no answer for a minute. But he called out after that pause, as he followed with the other portmanteau, 'Æsop coming! Jolly!' And then in a changed tone he said suddenly, 'How very unfortunate.'

I turned round and faced him as he sat upon the bed, and asked him what was unfortunate.

'At what time did you ask Æsop to be here?' he queried.

'Eight o'clock,' I answered.

'What a pity,' he said in an eager bustling way. 'I have an appointment I ought to have kept at once on coming into town.' He laid his hands on my shoulders, and put me away from him laughing. 'The pleasure of seeing you, Old Jack, sent it out of my

head; but I must keep it. I am a quarter
of an hour late already,' he went on, looking
at his watch. 'Let me write a line to Gregory, lest he should think I ran away from
him.'

I gave him pen, ink, and paper, and he
scrawled a hasty note. 'Read that,' he said,
as he threw it in an open envelope towards
me. 'I shall be back in an hour and a half
at latest.' He seized his hat, and was hurrying from the room, when I called after him.

'How about dinner?'

'Ah! dinner!' he said, turning with a hand
upon the door. 'Put it off till nine. Is
that possible? Or dine without me to-night.
Never mind, Old Jack. Better luck next
time.' With that he went out; and I heard
him leaping downstairs, two steps at a time.

He had not gone long when Gregory came
in. Gascoigne's sudden departure had left
me a little dull, and I was all the more rejoiced to see Æsop. He and I chatted in-
differently for a minute or two, until he said,
'You sent for me particularly. Anything up?'
I handed him Gascoigne's letter, thinking how
pleasant it would by-and-by for all three of
us to be together in my rooms. It was

growing dusk; and he took it to the window to read it. He seemed a long time getting through it, I thought, especially since Gascoigne had spent so little time in writing it. I asked at last if he did not find it legible. 'Yes,' he answered; 'legible enough. But it's very unlucky. I can't wait for him.'

'Can't wait for him?' I asked piteously. 'You take it very quietly, the two of you, spoiling my night in this way.'

'Ah, well,' said Æsop, with an air of philosophy; 'life's full of disappointments, and we must school ourselves to bear 'em.'

'Well, you'll come to-morrow, won't you? And we'll spend the day together.'

'Well, I'm not sure about to-morrow,' said Æsop, with an air of some constraint; 'but I'll write and tell you about it. Meantime, give the traveller drink; and I'll take a cigar. I've only half-an-hour to spare.'

Nothing remained but to make the best of it. I should have Gascoigne back directly, and a pleasant fortnight lay before me. Yet the rose-coloured bloom seemed somehow to be rubbed off that near future, and I felt quite chilled and unhappy. Gregory smoked his cigar almost in silence; and I went out with

him and saw him into a cab; and thereafter
went back to my chambers in a disconsolate
and gloomy mood, and awaited Gascoigne.

When he returned he heard of Gregory's
departure with so singular an absence of con-
cern in manner, though he said fluently enough
what a pity it was to miss Æsop, that I asked
him outright if he did not care to meet him.
He blushed a little, and said that all our youth-
ful friendships could scarcely be expected to
last as firmly as that between us two.   He
was so embarrassed whilst he said this, beneath the lightness of manner he assumed,
that before I had well thought it, I called
out, 'You don't care for Gregory.   Did
you leave me to avoid him?'

He turned quite red in his distress.   'Jack,'
he said appealingly, 'who has put such a
notion into your head?   Has Gregory hinted
anything of the kind?'

'No,' I cried; 'nothing.   It was only a fancy
of mine.   But I thought—you were both so
calm about missing each other—that you had
quarrelled, and did not wish me to know it.
You were not very much with each other at
Uncle Ben's place when you were down last,
and I have never seen you since, except apart.'

I thought he seemed relieved, though I could not conjecture why. He made no answer except to ask me if I had read his note to Gregory. When I said 'No,' he took it from the table where Gregory had left it, and handed it to me. It began, 'My dear Æsop,' and ended with, 'Yours always;' and there was no hint of anything but friendship in the few hearty lines which expressed his regret for keeping Gregory waiting.

There was no news from Gregory for four days; and I was so wounded at this, that it altogether dashed the triumph and pleasure of having Gascoigne to myself in my own London chambers; a matter which had seemed too pleasant to be real in the contemplation of it. On the morning of the fifth day, a letter came bearing the Paris post-mark, and expressing Æsop's regrets at his enforced absence. This cleared the cloud; for it explained that unexpected private business had sent him abroad. 'Assure Gascoigne of my best wishes,' said the letter at its close. 'There is no need to tell either of you how happy the réunion you planned would have made me, had it been possible for me to share in it.' So that there was no fear of any breach between them, I cared less for the absence of one of them.

Gregory did not return to town until Gascoigne had gone back to his curacy. I told him of the fears I had entertained about the possible decadence of their friendship ; and he listened to all I had to say with a solemnity very unusual with him. He spoke in answer with a sort of rough tenderness. 'You nurse illusions, young un. Heave 'em overboard ; but be sure you don't let your generous impulses go with 'em.'

He spoke so seriously, that I concluded he *had* a meaning ; though why the loss of any generous impulse should be involved in my ceasing to believe that he and Gascoigne had quarrelled, I could not divine. A sudden sound of footsteps on the staircase and a determined hammering at my outer door prevented the continuation of our talk ; and my visitors being admitted, made instant demands for drink, and stated that they had come with a proposal. They were amiable young people, with strong social leanings, and were supposed by their parents to be reading for the Bar. The proposal was that a convivial society should be formed, meeting in rotation at the

chambers of the men who belonged to it ; and
Gregory being voted to the chair, an initial
committee meeting was held. Bills of Wadham had come prepared with a suggestion
that the society should be known as ' The
Associated Order of Rum-Pum-Pahs and
Royal Brotherhood of Rollicking Rams ; '
and this imposing title being by acclamation
adopted, the rules and regulations of the
society were straightway framed. Jeans, late
of Exeter, and now of the Middle Temple,
barrister-at-law, called to that high profession
the week before last, was already glorious in
the possession of the services of a clerk, to
whom the task of engrossing the rules of the
new society was entrusted. We went for all
this genial nonsense with a certain solemnity
which became it well, and discussed laws and
by-laws with a business-like gravity which left
upon me a sense of having been hard at work.
The first meeting took place at my chambers,
and was attended by the consumption of much
liquid refreshment and a great number of
cigars. On this occasion I was formally in-
stalled as Royal Ram ; and Gregory was
created Deputy Royal Ram. A vast number of other offices were created, one of the

chief objects of the society being to include none who did not hold office within its ranks.

Thereafter, regular weekly meetings were held at the chambers of the various members ; and the society lived a flourishing and on the whole a very jovial and harmless life, which gave delight and hurt not. It reached an untimeous finish in the rooms in which it first came into being. The hour of midnight approached, and we were singing a chorus :

'From Wimbledon to Wombledon is seventeen miles ;
From Wombledon to Wimbledon is seventeen miles ;
From Wimbledon to Wombledon—
From Wombledon to Wimbledon—
From Wimbledon to Wombledon is seventeen miles.'

I had thought, in the pauses of this topographical record, that I could hear a knocking at the door ; and any doubt I might have had upon the point was set at rest when the end of the chorus came. Blows were dealt upon the door in a perfect shower, apparently by a heavy stick ; and one of my companions answering this noisy summons, reported the advent of 'an elderly Bloke in sportive raiment.' This announcement being made in a voice which must have been audible without, I went to greet my visitor, whoever he might be, with some reasonable dread that he might consider himself insulted. To my surprise, the visitor was no other than my Uncle Ben ; and before his eye caught mine, I could see both trouble and anger on his face.

'Come in, uncle,' I said, but with some awkwardness. 'I have a few friends here. I have told you about the Club in my letters, and it meets here to-night.'

He pushed by me without answer, and standing in the centre of the room, surveyed the assembly for a moment. Then nodding to Gregory, he removed his hat, and sat down in the chair I had occupied. 'Don't let me disturb your amusements,' he said gruffly ; but his angry countenance perturbed the young fellows, and they sat in silence, or talked to one another in subdued tones and formal phrases. In a little space one rose to go. Another followed him ; and in less than a quarter of an hour after Uncle Ben's arrival, the room was cleared. I had made an awkward presentation of my uncle to the assembly, and had tried to enter into talk with him ; but his manner, so different from anything I had hitherto observed in him, froze all geniality, and his answers were all a gloomy 'Yes' or

'No.' When at last the guests were all gone, he drank a tumbler of Burgundy, and rising, took his stand upon the hearthrug.

'What is the matter, uncle?' I asked, after a moment's pause, in which he had looked at me as if about to speak. 'Is any one ill at home? Is Maud—'

'I suppose,' he said, regarding me with a look of mingled grief and rage which, while it staggered, baffled me to understand—'I suppose you don't know of nothing as has took place, do you?'

'No,' I stammered—'unless it were the—'

'The what?' he asked me, with an almost fierce anxiety.

'The meeting here to-night, and the noise we were making when you came.'

He held his hat in his hand, and to my intense surprise, he dashed it, at this answer, on the floor, and broke into an execration. I regarded him with both amazement and fear; for the mood in which I saw him was so foreign to his nature, that I could only think him mad. Quite apart from the fact that he always drank with moderation, I could tell that he was sober now. He glared at me for full a minute with his face inflamed by rage; but he fought hard for self-control, and at last secured it.

'Anybody to look at you,' he said, 'ud think as you was wonder-struck.'

'I am indeed,' I answered. 'Pray, tell me what has happened.'

'Oh!' he said, shaking his head at me with an expression of bitter sorrow, 'you de- ceiver! Oh! you deceiver!'

'Uncle,' I cried, 'in what have I ever de- ceived you? What have I done?'

'You shall have a chance,' he said with a broken voice, whilst tears made their way to his eyes. 'I'll give you a opportunity. Make a clean breast of it, an' I'll overlook it.'

His appeal cut me to the quick; for I could read such a pathetic earnestness in his broken speech and his rugged homely face as I had never seen or heard elsewhere. But I had no answer. I was half giddy with surprise, and my mind was filled with quick-darting conjectures. All my guesses left me bewil- dered; for though I had a boyish fault and folly here and there set down in the books of conscience, I could think of nothing I had ever done or contemplated which seemed worthy of a tithe's tithe of his emotion.

'You shall have a chance,' he said. 'Tell me you done it. Tell me what you done it for. Promise me, on your sacred oath, as you'll never do it again, and this once I'll overlook it. Don't send your Uncle Ben off broken-hearted. Make a clean breast, an' I'll forgive you.' The tears were coursing down his face, and he spoke with a broken voice.

I think the love and sorrow which I felt for him steadied me. I answered then. 'Uncle, whatever suspicion you may harbour against me, I am innocent of having done one thing or thought one thought against your peace of mind. Tell me what you believe against me, and I will clear myself.'

'You're hardened,' he answered with returning anger; but my sister's blood's in you, and though your father was a rogue before you, I can't get over it. 'I can't believe,' he went on, softening again, 'as Bella's child's gone quite to the bad so young. Look here, Johnny. I took you for your mother's sake; an' I kep' you, an' I had you bred up like a gentleman, an' I did my best to make a man of you. If I seem to be stern with you, it's for your good. I can't overlook it, not without a full confession; an' even then, it'll take 'ears an' 'ears to overgrow it. But you clean your breast, an' I'll forgive you.'

'You quite bewilder me,' I answered earnestly. 'I know of nothing — I have done nothing, which could cause you such grief. Believe me, uncle, I would sooner die than even seem ungrateful.' In the eagerness of my protestation I approached him and laid a hand upon his arm; and he looked at me fixedly, whilst I could see sorrow again giving way to rage. Perhaps this alteration in his mood worked some change in mine; for I added with more firmness than I had been able hitherto to show, that I had a right to hear his accusation, and that it was impossible that I could clear myself until I knew of what I was suspected.

'Oh, you innocent, persecuted, wrong-suspected creature,' he cried with a bitter sneer. 'You haven't done nothin' mean, have you? You haven't done nothin' low, an' base, an' blackguardly, an' criminal, have you now? Law bless us' no; he wouldn't.'

'I have not,' I cried, with mounting anger at the obstinacy of his accusation, and his refusal to put it before me plainly. 'And whoever charges such a thing against me, lies.'

'What?' he said again. 'You've made your mind up to brave it out, an' swear black's white?'

'Neither your past tenderness to me,' I answered, 'nor your relationship, nor your age, gives you a right to speak so. If you have any charge to bring, speak it out. If you will give me no chance to clear myself, I will not listen to your accusations.' Those were the last words I spoke to him; for he broke out with a wild exclamation, and struck me across the face so heavily that I fell and lay unconscious for a time. When I awoke, dizzily and painfully, there was already a grey light peering through the windows, and I was alone. The interview with Uncle Ben seemed at first like a miserable dream; but as it cleared itself to my memory, nothing but wounded pride withheld my tears.

CHAPTER V.

HISTORY.

' He had no change in her remembrance.'

A N English novelist of great genius says,
in taking leave of the chief female
figure of his story :—' Such women are not
the spice of fiction, but they are the salt of
real life.' That phrase expresses so exactly
what I feel and desire to say of Maud, that
I should probably have used it originally, if
Charles Reade had not forestalled me. Did
it ever occur to you to think that the especial
charm and beauty of some women is—that
they have suffered? The esteem and liking
with which you regard them, even in your
days of strangerhood, and before the usages
of friendship have endeared them, is instinc-
tive. The chivalry of the manly heart is
awakened at the thought of such unmerited

trouble as the faces of many good women unconsciously tell of. There is a look almost angelic in such faces; the gentle eyes that would fain smile kindly on all things, have been made familiar with tears; yet they still smile, a little wistfully maybe, but tenderly—the very twilight of a smile—no garish brilliance that blinds and dazzles, but a sad and gentle light, which soothes the soul as an autumn evening sky will, and disposes the heart to a quiet and reverent peace.

If old Time, whom we figure with scythe and hour-glass, had but a real personality, how should we sing his praises, how tell our thanks to him? Good old FATHER Time, who dost bear us in fatherly arms away from sorrows, away from all sorrows in a while, if we will but have a little patience!

Maud in these days dwelt in peace. I have no skill to tell how the peace came down, and settled round about her like strong sunshine, until at last she would scarcely for her own sake have recalled her sorrow. Had that harrowing mystery which had first belonged to her lover's fate still seemed to hang over it, things might have gone otherwise with her, and peace might at least have been delayed. But she had learned that he was dead, and that his unknown griefs were over; and it came to pass that poor Frank's best hopes were justified, and she found rest. She did not forget him, and will not, though she should live to be old, cease to remember her first lover with infinite sad sweetness of remembrance and tender pity. The cares which a good woman can lay upon herself for the cares of other people soothed and gladdened her, and she moved among the poor like a ministering angel. Poor rural folk are not so susceptible to gratitude as it might be wished they should be; but she took root in the shallow hearts of her old women, who grumbled to her over their rheumatics and their old men and the hardness of the parish, 'which ud only give 'em a loaf a week, an' times that hard.' These crabbed old creatures used to talk of her to each other, and though they knew little enough of her trouble, would say 'Poor dear!' when they mentioned her, by a sort of pitying instinct, which perhaps her eyes inspired.

Will Fairholt, though touched always by that casuist fear which he had long since expressed to Hastings, found the definite news of his brother's death a relief to him. It was a great grief; for, as we have seen, he had a sincere love for Frank; but he felt, when the first wound of loss was healed, happier and more at ease than he had done for many and many a week before the news reached him. I have not time to tell the whole story of his healing; but as even in a river on its hurrying way to the sea you may find a quiet back-water here and there, where foam of haste and voice of ripple are not, so my story, which serves a less important use than any river, may pause awhile, and we may suffer ourselves to fall into that calm bay in which the lives of these two, after much tempestuous tossing to and fro, have found shelter.

'My life has been but a poor business, Maud,' said Will one day as he walked by her side in the gardens at Hartley Hall. Before them was the gate at which she and Frank had stood together years ago when they parted as pledged lovers. The day was warm and bright and drowsy, and the shadows were growing long towards the east. 'My life has been but a poor business. For I have spent years out of the world idly, which should have been spent within it busily. I have never dared to name the purpose which has kept me here, and I have been living in a fool's paradise for years.'

'How?' she said, looking up at him frankly and openly, with questioning eyes.

'I had no right,' he said, 'to trap you into such a question. And I did not mean it.' She understood him then, and almost knew everything he had yet to say. Do you remember when you .first came here, and poor Frank and I first saw you?'

'I remember well,' she answered softly.

'I can remember,' he went on, 'no hour since then in which you have not been the centre of my life. Did you ever guess that?'

'I knew it,' she said softly; 'and I was very sorry.'

'You know it now,' he continued, bending over her. 'Are you still sorry?' She gave no answer, but hung her head a little. 'I have loved you nearly all my life. Maud, can you give me a little hope?'

'I am very sorry,' she began, and his heart failed within him; but her voice went on tremulously, 'that you have —' And there she paused again.

' That I have spoken ? ' he asked.

' That you have suffered so,' she answered more boldly, lifting her head and meeting his eyes with hers. As she faced him thus, a tender blush stole over the delicate pallor of her countenance, and it was not easy to endure the ardent question of his eyes.

He stretched out his hands and took both of hers unresisting. ' I have thought,' he said, ' I have hoped that our partnership in a common grief might bring us nearer to each other ; though if I know my heart, I schooled myself to see your happiness, and to live apart from you without repining.'

' Will,' she said, as if entreating him, ' I knew it all—I knew it all.'

' But I have waited,' he went on, 'hoping against hope that time might heal your grief, and make a standing-place for me beside you. I have waited long, Maud, long, long ! But have I waited long enough ?'

Her eyes faltered downward whilst he spoke ; but she raised them again and looked him bravely in the face, though they were dim with tears. He saw then that no further speech was needed, and folded her to his heart.

They were middle-aged people, and the passionate raptures and delights of young love were out of reach. But as I have known the delirious happiness of youth breed a sort of heart-vertigo, so I have seen courtship in a man of forty and a woman of four-and-thirty full of very solid happiness. As for Maud, it was not the young love, but it was enough for happiness; for she pitied and esteemed her lover, and had had the most constant and tender friendship for him for many years. And there was this singular factor in the case, as a matter of distinct feeling, although as a thing of course one conscious thought would have ousted it — that whereas she had passed the first bloom of her womanhood, Frank was still and for ever and always a bright, handsome, wilful lad. He had no change in her remembrance. She grew towards middle age; but his figure was no sturdier, his open brow took no corroding wrinkles, his voice had the ring of jolly youth in it. The deep maternal instinct in the heart of an old maid awoke, and she claimed this perennial youth for her child, not her lover. How should he be her lover, the bright, dandified, clever young fellow, who had grown no older this sixteen years ; whilst grief had wasted her bloom, and time had reconciled her ! Infinitely sad and sweet and tender were these memories, like a mother's remembrances of her child. For, ah ! the dead who die young are always young, until we, who cherish their memory, follow them.

Will was quietly contented. There was no great excitement in his joy. As we near forty, most of us are disposed to take the delights of life soberly. Your 'wild and wanton colts, fetching mad bounds, neighing and bellowing,' are pleasant to look at, typifying youth and high spirits ; but the trained steed who finds himself fetlock-deep in sweet grass, has a placid rest and ease in the sense that his burden is away, which are perhaps as satisfactory to him as the more demonstrative joys of colthood used to be. Will had borne his burden manfully, waited his time with patience, and accepted his happiness with a glad solemnity of thanksgiving.

Neither she nor he felt any wish to talk just then. They strolled slowly on to the gate together, and looked out over the park, where the peaceful sunlight lay among the trees, and the distance shimmered a little, as

if the air were alive between and breathed
gently in the heat. Then they turned and
strolled back in happy silence to the house,
and parted there ; and Will strayed down to
the arbour behind the rhododendron walk,
where Mr. Hartley mostly loved to take
his ease. The old man was asleep, with a
yellow bandana handkerchief over his head ;
and his hands were peacefully folded over
his waistcoat, which was a little more bulkily
projected than it had used to be. Will sat
down and lit a cigar, and waited till the old
boy should awake. He had pleasant thoughts
for his companions, and was in no hurry ; but
a sound of yawning made itself heard from
under the yellow bandana ; one hand went
lazily up and removed the silken screen ; and
Benjamin Hartley observing his companion,
nodded at him idly and good-humouredly,
closed his eyes for a few more seconds,
yawned again, reopened his eyes, smoothed
his legs with his hands, and said finally in a
voice of lazy comfort, 'Well, Mr. William,
how goes it ?'

'It goes very well indeed,' said Will, smil-
ing ; 'and only needs your hand to push it into
smooth water.'

'Eh?' said Mr. Hartley, sitting up with a bewildered face.

'Maud and I, Mr. Hartley—' Will began in explanation.

'Ah!' said Mr. Hartley with an appreciative grin.

'Have made up our minds that we care for each other. But there is a Wicked Uncle in the case, as there has been in the stories of many young people' [Mr. Hartley's smile, appreciative of the situation, grew wider]— 'and it is necessary to soothe him, and obtain his sanction.'

'He's a hard old beast that there uncle, Mr. William,' said Mr. Hartley with a joyful wink. 'But if you was to go at him together, I think you'd manage him.'

'I think we should,' Will answered. 'But I want to pave the way by which we must approach him.'

'You come along of me,' said the Wicked Uncle; and Will throwing away his cigar, walked with him to the house, where the old man went in search of Maud; and having found her brought her on his arm. 'Mr. William,' he said, not without dignity, 'I've known you, good man and true English

gentleman, for twenty year. I never knowed
a thing about you as could make you unworthy of my girl; and as I find her willin',
I give her to you with all my heart. And
she knows what I think about her—don't
you, my dear?' With that he kissed her
heartily, and then put her hand in Will's;
and posing with high glee with both hands
aloft, said, 'Bless you, my children!' in a
manner so jovially pompous and absurd, that
even Maud laughed. Mr. Hartley for his
part shouted with a somewhat suspicious
hilarity. 'Bless your heart, my dear,' he
said to Maud, 'do you know as I've took to
novel-reading in my old age, and plays, and
them sort o' things? I know all the proper
sentimental dodges now.—Stop to dinner, Mr.
William?—No? All right—as you like. I'm
a-going back to the arbour, I am, to finish
the nap as you two young uns broke into
with your love-making.' The good old
heathen rolled back to his arbour a little
sadly, and sat there a long time lonely, until
Will had taken leave of Maud and came out
to join him.

'You will be lonely when I am gone,' she
said, after an affectionate talk.

'No,' the old man answered stoutly; 'I sha'n't be nothing of the sort. An' you'll come and live here, half the year at least. That I *do* expect.' He stroked her hair, as he had used to do when she was a child, and patted her cheek.

'You are a good, unselfish uncle,' she answered fondly.

He stroked her hair still, and answered, 'If I was one of them book-writing fellers, my dear, I'd write a tale.'

'Yes,' said she; 'and what would it be, uncle?'

'It 'ud be about two different people; an' I'd make one of 'em a grinding, selfish blackguard, don't you see; and I'd make th' other a man as 'd act fair even if he lost by it. An' I should show folks as the man as allays tried to be happy was miserable; an' I should show 'em as the man as acted fair an' generous was happy in the long-run, even when he lost. Supposing I'd ha' said, " No; stop with me," you'd ha' stopped—wouldn't you?'

'Yes,' she answered; 'I should have stayed.'

'Now, look there!' he said. 'What a conscience I should ha' carried! You'd ha' seen me a-going about like a regular Misery. I

know you'd ha' stayed, my dear. I know you
would. An' I should ha' brought my own grey
hairs down with sorrow to the grave. Not as
there's many of 'em,' said the good old fellow,
polishing his baldness with his handkerchief,
'nor hasn't been this many a 'ear. No, no,
no, my dear,' he went on, answering his own
thoughts. 'It's old age's happiness to see
them as they love happy. I'm a very happy
man, my darlin'—a very happy man. Every-
thin' 's prospered with me wonderful. I've
got a lot to be thankful for, an' happy over.
Theer's the Major—he's a credit to me ; ain't
he now ? Theer's 'Orace—he's a credit to me.
Feller of his college, an' as stately a gentleman as ever was. Makes me half afraid to
look at him ; but he's a good son, Maud,
an' never caused me a day's trouble in his
life. Then theer's Johnny. He's a good lad,
my dear ; ain't he now ? No harm in him.
A quiet, upright, honourable lad. Then
theer's you, a-going to be happy. Why, bless
my soul,' said Mr. Hartley, with a melancholy
effort to be genial, 'wheer is there a happier
man than me ?' With that he kissed her ;
and she felt his tears warm upon her face.
But she knew that there was no more bitter-

ness in them than in her own ; and when he
had unaffectedly dried his eyes with his yellow
handkerchief and kissed her once more, they
rose together, and walked towards the house
in a tranquil and tender peace, which I feel it
no sin to envy.

It had been Will Fairholt's intention to lay
his purpose before his father at once ; but the
old gentleman was in so irritable and testy
a mood that he deemed it wise to postpone
his revelation till the morrow. So, on a sunny
morning, when Mr. Fairholt was strolling
slowly and with difficulty up and down his
favourite walk in the shrubbery, Will joined
him, and began, ' I think it my duty, sir, to ask
your consent in a matter of great importance.'

' What is that ?'

' I hope shortly to be married, and— '

' You ought to have married long ago,' Mr.
Fairholt said testily. ' It's a hard thing for
a man to feel that he is the last but one of
his house, in the male line. Who is it ? Is
it that girl of Hartley's ?'

' It is Mr. Hartley's niece,' said Will simply.
He was used to his father's manner, and made
large allowances for him, thinking how much
he had suffered.

'I thought so,' the old man answered, re-
senting an injury as usual. 'You will please
yourself, of course. The estate's entailed, and
goes to you ; and I have neither part nor lot,
nor influence either, for that matter, in the
whole affair.'

'I have never crossed you knowingly, father,'
Will said gently.

'No,' said Mr. Fairholt captiously ; 'you've
been a good son to me, Will, a good son. And
I've no fault to find with the girl. A girl she's
not any longer ; but you're not a boy any longer,
and I have no fault to find. Her uncle is
vulgar—vulgar to his finger-ends ; but she has
a well-bred look and manner. I don't care to
approach the fellow again ; but I suppose I
shall have to see him now. That sort of man
is vulgar in soul, Will, that self-made, money-
grubbing sort of man. I have met people of
no family—when I was younger, and mixed
with the world—whose manners had no trace
of polish, and who were yet not intolerable.
That fellow Hartley is a bear. The man's
heart is wrong, and the vileness of his manner
is a natural consequence. His son is a par-
venu ; that — that army fellow, quite a bad
imitation of a gentleman. I don't know much

about the girl; but people speak well of her. Young Borroleigh, Chesterwood's son, wanted to marry her, I remember, nearly a dozen years ago. Money, I suppose; though he ought to have enough of it. Chesterwood has been stingy enough these thirty years. I'm told that poor Frank was attached to her. Yes, yes; you have my consent, if you want it. Let me be alone a little while now. I am tired of talking.' And he fell to wondering, as he paced feebly up and down the shrubbery walk in the morning sunshine, how much the millionaire would give his niece. 'I'll see him about it,' he said—'I'll see him about it. Will's quite a fool in money matters—quite a fool. Gad, he shall gild the pill, any-way!' And he laughed a little at that comfortable reflection.

It was perhaps not a remarkable thing that at the same moment Benjamin Hartley should have been thinking in the same strain—with a reverse of persons. 'I shall have to gild the pill,' he said to himself, 'an' gild it pretty thick too, into the bargain, to get old Fairholt to swaller it without makin' a wry face. Well, well; it'll only be a flea-bite out o' the Major's share an' 'Orace's. I suppose I could buy the proud old rascal up, an' scarcely know I'd done it.' So that it seemed fairly probable that Mr. Fairholt's desire to have the pill gilded would not be difficult of fulfilment.

It was decided that the marriage should not be long delayed ; and the negotiations between family pride and Mammon were conducted without hitch or hindrance. But a week or two before the time originally appointed for the wedding, Fate dealt Benjamin Hartley a terrible blow. There came into his hands a cheque bearing the endorsement of his sister's son, John Campbell, and a forged copy of his own signature, so close that he himself was almost deceived by it. 'Pay John Campbell, Esq., or Order, Two Hundred Pounds.' His mingled grief and rage almost drove him mad. He had treated the boy with fatherly tender-ness and generosity ; and the inexplicable base-ness and ingratitude of this return bade fair to break his heart. He went heart-brokenly to his solicitors and conferred with the leading partner, to whom he told the story.

'What do you propose to do?' asked the lawyer. 'Shall you prosecute?'

Mr. Hartley glared at him with indignation ; almost with contempt. 'No!' he said; 'I sha'n't prosecute; and I sha'n't plunge the miserable young scoundrel into crime. I want you to send for him, and to tell him what I know; for though I tried last night, I couldn't bring myself to frame the words and say 'em to him. Tell him that you've got my instructions to invest five thousand pounds for him. That'll go to buy a practice when he's got a diploma, and meantime it can bear interest at five per cent., and he can live on the interest. It ain't what I meant to do by him; but it's more than he deserves.'

'Much more,' said the lawyer. 'If I might advise—'

'You needn't,' said Mr. Hartley, with a sort of weary anger. 'If he's got any debts, pay 'em. Tell him if he writes to me I shall send his letters back unopened. Tell him I've done with him, beyond this, for good and all. Here,' he added suddenly, drawing the forged cheque from his pocket-book; 'show him that.' He threw it on the table, whence it fell to the floor. The lawyer stooped and picked it up; and the millionaire said drearily, 'Don't say nothing about me, except as these is my instructions. But I wouldn't ha' had it done by him, Bilton, not if I'd lost every penny I'm worth. Good-

bye, Bilton. You've got my will. Make the
ne'ssary alterations in it; and send somebody
down with it for me to sign. And be quick
about it; for I don't think, Bilton, as I shall
last much longer.'

'For many a year, I hope,' said the lawyer;
but Benjamin Hartley, shaking his head sadly
went away with his hopes all dashed. He
carried a heavy heart into the country; and
was for a long time so ailing that Maud's
marriage was deferred; and where everything
had lately been so happy, all was turned to
gloom.

CHAPTER VI.

AUTOBIOGRAPHY.

' Are you willing to submit to that arbitrament.'

IT may be allowed to go without saying that
the day after Uncle Ben's last visit to me
was very miserable, and that I was in a state
of the cruellest perplexity. I could neither
eat nor sleep, and I locked myself in my
chambers, and spent the time alone. The only
thing I could definitely resolve upon was to
write to Maud, beseeching her, for pity's sake,
to discover the ground of my uncle's mysterious
accusations, and to allow me a chance of
clearing myself. I wrote a lengthy letter, and
posted it in the darkness of the night; and
feeling a little relieved, went back to my
chambers, where I tried in vain to sleep. In
the morning, when my laundress was laying
the cloth for breakfast, and I was hiding in

the bedroom, to conceal from her the bruise upon my face which resulted from the blow I had received, I heard a step upon the stairs, and a minute later a pert voice asked for me. I had not given the laundress instructions to deny me, anticipating no visitor at that early hour, and she announced that I was in.

'A gentleman to see you, sir,' she said a moment later, tapping at my door.

'Who is it?' I asked.

'From Bilton, Bilton, and Hart, sir,' said the pert voice, and a young man, with a crimson tie, and a general burlesque of fashion in air and dress, came into my bedroom with his hat in his hand. 'I am the bearer of a letter, sir,' he said with an airy flourish, 'from our principal. I trust it is not of overwhelming importance, but I was instructed to deliver it last night.'

I took the letter and read it. It said briefly that the writer, my uncle's solicitor, was instructed by him to seek an interview with me, and that it was desirable that it should take place as soon as possible. Trusting that some explanation would be given of the scene which had so painfully bewildered me, I asked the young man in the crimson tie at what hour

it would probably be convenient for Mr. Bilton
to see me. He replied that the principal was
always at the office 'from ten in the morning
up to any hour at night, as it might happen,'
and being told to say that I would follow him
at once, he gradually abstracted himself from
the contemplation of his figure in the looking-
glass which fronted the central door of a large
wardrobe, and went his way. After a visit
to a chemist in the Strand, who had especial
skill in the disguising of facial damages, I took
a cab to Holborn, and, forgetting to discharge
the man, went into the office of my uncle's
lawyers, and was shown at once into the room
of the senior partner, whom I had seen once
before in my uncle's company. I offered to
shake hands with him, but he nodded towards a
seat, and asked me to take it. I sat down, and
prepared as calmly as I could to listen.

'Mr. Hartley was here yesterday,' he began.
' He tells me that you deny all knowledge of
the case against you, and since he feels the
disgrace of it too deeply to enter into any
conversation with you concerning it, he has
deputed me to—in short to lay the proof of
your guilt before you.'

I have often heard and read that an innocent

man charged with crime is supported by the consciousness of his own rectitude. I believe that to be rather more foolish than most generalisations; and I know that when the lawyer spoke in so calm and assured a fashion, I was almost beaten into the belief that I had committed some awful crime, though I had quite forgotten what it was.

'Do you know that signature?' he asked, holding a piece of paper across the table.

'Yes,' I answered, as calmly as I could. 'It is mine.'

'Is that yours also?' he questioned, turning the paper round and showing the heavy autograph of Benjamin Hartley. I looked inquiry at the lawyer; and he, returning my gaze fixedly, tapped the paper three or four times with his finger. 'Is that your handwriting, young gentleman?' he asked again.

'No,' I answered, confused and irritated by a question so seriously put and so palpably absurd. 'That is my uncle's writing.'

'Ah!' he said, 'will you tell me when Mr. Hartley gave you this cheque for two hundred pounds?'

I began to see the form the accusation was

about to take. At least I think it was then
that I began to see it ; but I was quite con-
founded and amazed. 'Tell me the date,'
I asked at last ; remembering that I had in
my pocket a memorandum of all my receipts
from Uncle Ben within the last three or four
years. He gave me the date, and I looked
along my list. There was no such date
there, and there was no sum of two hundred
pounds set down. There were two of two
hundred and fifty, and several of a hundred.
I passed the pocket-book, with my finger on
the open page, across to the lawyer.

'Ah !' he said again shortly ; 'you didn't
enter this.'

'I never received it,' I made answer.

'I am sure you didn't,' he responded.
'The fact, is, sir, that you forged this
cheque.'

For just a second, my one impulse was to
knock Mr. Bilton down. That passed, and
I was conscious of nothing except a giddy
rage against the supposition that such a belief, however substantiated, could be held concerning me, and a sort of rebellious loathing
of it. I knew that the lawyer was talking,
but I had no conception as to what he said ;

and it was after a silence that I asked with a throbbing heart to be allowed to look at the cheque once more. 'You had better be sure,' he said, with a sort of scornful bitterness, 'that it is the one you forged.'

That stung me, and I answered hotly, 'You are insolent, Mr. Bilton. When next you have a business of this kind in hand, be sure before you speak so.' He shrugged his shoulders and raised his eyebrows, and made a little motion with his hands. His gesture and expression gave me leave, more scornfully than words would have done, to take what tone I pleased. I dared scarcely trust my eyes upon him in the anger to which this stirred me, and I took up the cheque and feigned to examine it anew.

'Mr. Hartley,' he said then, in a quiet, measured way, 'instructs me to tell you that he will hold no further communication with you ; but that since he does not desire to drive you into further crime, he will make an allowance of two hundred and fifty pounds a-year to you whilst your studies continue, and that this will be—'

'Do you think,' I cried passionately, 'that if my uncle believes *this* of me,' and I struck the cheque as it lay upon the table, 'that I will take another penny from him?'

'This,' he went on quietly in the same formal tone, reaching out for the cheque as he spoke and smoothing it out on the desk before him, ' will be the interest of a lump sum which will be devoted at the close of your career as a student to the purchase of a professional practice. If you have any debts, you will instruct your tradesmen to send in their bills to me. I shall examine them closely, and shall pay them. Beyond this, you have nothing to expect from Mr. Hartley; and had he taken my advice, he would have left you to your own resources, even if he had not proceeded against you.'

'I am obliged to you,' I answered, as suddenly hard and cold as if boiling lava had been changed to ice. If that simile should seem extravagant, let it pass. It seems true enough, in my recollection. 'Will you kindly write to Mr. Hartley, and tell him that so long as he retains this shameful suspicion of me, I shall not trouble him? Will you say that I decline to receive a farthing from his hands? Say, if you please, that it shall be the one aim of my life to repay him the money he has expended upon me. Tell him that this charge, so made, without inquiry, without appeal to me, without effort to trace the criminal who has made use of his name and mine, wipes out all gratitude, affection, and regard, and that we are no more to each other now than creditor and debtor. We shall hold those relations not an hour longer than I can help.'

'You brave it out,' he said, as I turned to go.

'Do you consider,' I asked him, 'that you are giving me fair-play? Are you acting honourably in this matter, or like a gentleman? I claim to be held innocent until my guilt is proved. I tell you, sir, that my name has been forged as well as my uncle's. I will protect myself in this matter, and I can see no other course than to put the whole affair into the hands of the police. If, in the meantime, I am suspected, I cannot help it.'

I could see even as I turned to go that a change came over his face, and that he looked less scornful and less confident. 'Stop!' he said. 'Are you willing to submit to that arbitrament?'

I answered 'Yes;' and in obedience to his gesture, resumed my seat.

He wrote a note, rang the bell, and despatched a clerk with the missive, giving him
instructions to wait for an answer, and to return if possible with the man.

'You have sent for a police officer?' I asked
him.

'I have sent,' he answered, 'for a private
detective.'

I waited for more than an hour. A clock
upon the mantel-piece had that irritating im-
portunity in its voice which belongs to all
timepieces when one is silent and waiting.
Mr. Bilton sorted papers, wrote letters, made
notes on the edges of documents. I watched
him stonily, and listened to the ticking of the
clock. Sometimes everything was so quiet
that I could hear the scratching of a clerk's
quill in the next room, or the rustle of a
foolscap sheet as it was turned. At length
the private dectective came—a little man dressed
in black, and looking something like an under-
taker. He bowed to us both, and took his
seat with his hat suspended by the rim between
his knees.

'This young gentleman,' said Mr. Bilton,
pointing the feather of a quill towards me, 'is
the nephew of Mr. Hartley the millionaire.'—

The detective nodded. — 'His uncle, Mr. Hartley, has received this cheque from his bankers, and proclaims the signature a forgery. It is made payable, you see, to John Campbell, Esq. This'—indicating me again—'is John Campbell, Esq. The cheque, observe, is indorsed "John Campbell," and it has been cashed at the bank. Mr. Hartley believes that Mr. Campbell has forged his signature. Mr. Campbell protests that some other person has forged both Mr. Hartley's signature and his. Now, you will undertake to keep this gentleman in sight; but if he can give you any clue, you must bring it to me, and we will act upon it. You will make what you can of the case, for Mr. Campbell or against him. In either result, you will look to me for payment. You had better take the cheque; and you can report to me as soon as you have formed your opinion.'

'I am, then,' I said, rising, 'to consider myself under surveillance?'

'Until,' he answered, 'your innocence is established, or you are arrested upon this charge.'

'You will act upon your own authority, if I am arrested?' I asked.

'I shall be able to justify my proceedings in the proper quarter, I have no doubt.' He said no more; and I left him there. The detective came with me down-stairs and walked beside me in the street. The cabman I had left waiting outside hailed me, and I asked the detective to accompany me home. The journey was made in absolute silence; and when my rooms were reached, and the laundress, who was still pottering helplessly about them, had been dismissed, I sat down to an examination of the case, with all the detective's experience to help me.

'Do you know anything about handwritings?' I asked him. Well, he made answer, that depended. Did he think he could detect a forgery—a clever forgery—if he had the real handwriting and the false before him? Yes, he said: he'd bet all he was worth, he could. I laid before him several examples of my own signature, and asked him to compare them with the endorsment of the cheque. He did so, and ended by pronouncing them to be identical. I looked at them for myself, and could perceive no difference. I had letters of my uncle's, and produced them. We laid the signatures of those letters side by side with the forgery of my uncle's name; and though the imitation was painstaking and wonderfully accurate, we both thought we could detect a difference between the real and the false.

'I'm not a professional expert,' said the detective, who was unpleasantly familiar and free in manner: 'but I've studied this business, and I'll lay my life I'm right. *That's* a forgery,' pointing to the signature; 'and that'—turning the cheque over to look again at the endorsement—' is the real handwriting.'

This was depressing; and I seemed so hedged round by the perplexity and misery of the whole business, that I knew not what to do or say. I begged him at last to take a professional expert's opinion; and he promised that he would do so; though I could see only too clearly that he was persuaded of my guilt, and believed that I was playing a stubborn game in pretence of ignorance.

'Perhaps,' he said, 'you won't mind obliging me by coming to see a man I know, at once?'

I told him I should be glad to go with him to do anything. But I discovered later on that his only purpose was not to lose sight of me; for after having taken me to a house, which I afterwards discovered to be his own, and having kept me waiting there in an office hung round with photographs of people, he feigned to make further inquiries, and to discover that there was no chance of seeing the expert that day. He had knocked at his own door when we arrived at it, and had inquired for this fictitious expert so innocently and naturally, and the man who answered the door had fallen into his plot so smoothly, that I had no suspicion until afterwards of the trick he had played me; though I was not long in discovering the fact that a very seedy man, who nourished a perennial sore throat in four or five yards of dirty red comforter, had been set to watch me.

I was sitting miserably in my chambers two or three days later, when Gregory came in, and was surprised to see me looking so ill and dejected. I had much ado not to burst out in tears whilst I told the story; but I succeeded in telling it; and he, assuring me of his unchanged and unchangeable faith in me, cheered me a good deal. After some declamation against the wretchedness of this suspicion, which his sympathy encouraged me to make, I flagged again, until Æsop startled me by slapping the table with his hand. I looked up, and he said cheerfully, 'Young un, attend to me.'—I signified attention ; and he continued, business-like, 'You tell me you can't find any difference between this forged signature and your own ?'

'None,' I said.

'And your uncle and his lawyer, who are both observant men, can't find any ?'—I shook my head.—'And the detective can't find any ?' —I shook my head again.—'Suppose then that there isn't any ? Suppose you have been trapped into writing your name upon that cheque ? Is there a chance of that ?'

No ; I saw none. But at his command, I went with him in search of the detective, whom we found at home in the room hung with photographs, where he was smoking a cigarette with his feet upon the table. He touched with his forefinger the peaked cap he wore, and his whole demeanour was marked by an appearance of a sense that he was master of the situation. This became so apparent when Gregory had asked and the detective had answered some half-dozen questions, that Æsop came down upon him with grave satire.

'You are requested definitely to understand, Mr. Latazzi,' said Æsop, 'that you are wanted to inquire into this case. Your preconceived opinion as to its merits is not the thing paid for, or desired. We wish you to bend your intellect to the facts. When you have done that, you can form as many theories as you like.'

'Very good,' said the detective, who was a man of imperturbable phlegm. 'Come to the facts.'

'The first fact is that you have the cheque in your possession. Oblige me by allowing me to look at it,'

'Mr. Latazzi took his feet from the table, and strolled to a safe, which he unlocked and flung open with a flourish. He produced the cheque, and resumed his old position and his cigarette, after relocking the safe. Gregory having regarded the document closely, asked the detective how many handwritings there were upon it. Mr. Latazzi answered—two. How did he divide them? Æsop demanded.

'The "John Campbell, Esq.," the "two hundred pounds," the date and the figures, are written by one hand; and the signature and the indorsement by another.'

'You are sure that the signature and the indorsement are by one hand?'

'Mr Campbell wrote them both,' the detective answered quietly. I could not say that the manner of this speech was insolent, but it was not unnatural that I was angered by it.

Gregory waved me back when I would have advanced. 'Does your uncle commonly write his cheques on plain paper, Jack?'

'I never saw a cheque of his so written,' I responded.

'Your uncle is a business man, isn't he? For instance, he looks over his bank-book pretty regularly, and checks his cash account, and all that sort of thing, and looks over the paid cheques returned to him by his bankers.'

'He is the most methodical man I ever knew.'

'He was dead certain to find this forgery out, I suppose?'

'I cannot think,' I answered, 'that there could have been a possibility of its escaping him.'

'How much has he spent on you during the last year?'

I gave twelve hundred pounds as an approximate estimate.

'You believe, Mr. Latazzi,' said Æsop, 'that

my friend would choose a common scrap of
paper like this on which to forge a cheque,
when he knew that Mr. Hartley never used
a plain cheque? You believe further that one
who could forge as cleverly as this '—laying
his finger on the imitation of my uncle's
massive signature—' would be so lazy and so
blind as not to take the trouble to forge another name at the back of it, but would stick
his own there, and run his neck into a noose
by doing it? Are those your theories?'

'If you come to me to ask my help and
advice,' said the detective, 'it might be as well,
sir, to come to me civilly. If you know more
than I do about the matter, you can manage it
yourself.'

'Then we will manage it ourselves,' said
Gregory; and we left the office, Mr. Latazzi
with great calm puffing at his cigarette behind
us to the door. 'Who are the experts in
handwriting, Jack? British or foreign, metro-
politan or provincial; let us have the beggars
up to judgment. That pig-headed villain is
no detective. No man who theorises has a
right to call himself a detective. Come along
Jack, to the great house of English police
intelligence opposite Whitehall. Let us con-

sult the great Defective Force, miscalled detective. We'll ask one question : Who are the experts ? and then we'll ask another : Where do they live ? And then, sir, we will have done with the Defective Force for the time being. — Detective !' said Æsop, savagely. 'That fellow call himself a detective ! The man's ugly vanity has stared him in the face all his life, huge as a pyramid, and he hasn't detected *that*.' Talking thus, half in real heat of anger, and half, as I surmised, for my awaking, he strode on towards the nearest cab-stand. We spent the greater part of that day in driving about London in search of the three men who at that time were known to fame and the police authorities as experts in handwriting. With a great deal of difficulty we got them to undertake to meet together at Mr. Bilton's office on the following day ; and late in the evening we ourselves drove thither just in time to find the senior partner leaving. I had scarce told Æsop who the lawyer was, when my friend went impetuously at him, and explained with great ardour but close-cut brevity the course he had taken, and begged to be allowed to summon Mr. Latazzi to produce the cheque. Mr. Bilton, who had taken us into the clerk's office to hear Gregory's statement, promised to send for the detective; let us out again, and bade us a grave goodnight.

Gregory dined with me, and my spirits rose almost to fever-heat; but at his departure the flame of hope flickered, and almost went out. It rose again next morning when he came; and I went down to Holborn with him in a pitiable flutter of nervous excitement, bearing with me a bundle of manuscripts of my own, and several letters of my uncle's. The experts met; and Æsop and I awaited their decision in the parlour of an hotel near at hand. After the expiration of a dreary time — the three hours seemed like three weeks to me — the clerk who had borne Mr. Bilton's letter came to summon us; and I remember distinctly how I thought that he must hear the pulses beating riotously in my head as he walked behind us.

'Your friend has done something for you, Mr. Campbell,' said the lawyer. 'Two of the experts are of opinion that the forgery of Mr. Hartley's signature is not yours.'

'Will you write to that effect to Mr. Hartley?' I asked in great agitation.

'One of the experts gives his word against you,' said Mr. Bilton, who was simply business-like, and had no more emotion in the matter than if it had been the most trivial in the world. 'But we have set Latazzi upon a new track. If you are innocent, you will be cleared.'

'But,' I urged, 'it is cruel alike to my uncle and myself to withhold the result of this examination from him. The balance of evidence is on my side, and I have a right to ask that he should know it.'

'Your uncle, Mr. Campbell,' returned the lawyer, 'would not resign his opinion for all the experts in the world. We must have more than this to move him. And he is a most valued friend of mine, sir, and I will not agitate him by a hope which even yet might prove fallacious. I do not say it will, I say it *might*. Do you know how much we know about this matter? We know that the paper upon which the cheque was written came from your chambers; and we have even been so fortunate as to secure, through Mr. Gregory, its fellow half-sheet from your waste-paper basket. We know through the same source that the indorsement is written in the ink you habitually use, as it is certainly your signature, and that the writing on the other side is in a different fluid. We shall make inquiries at the bank ; and we shall discover who presented the cheque, and where he went. In short, sir, we know much already which tends to clear you ; and I believe we shall shortly know something which will crimi-nate somebody else. But you cannot yet be regarded as free from suspicion, and I should recommend patience.'

I went back to my chambers in very low spirits, and there endeavoured to exercise patience to such effect that in three days I lay in a raging fever.

CHAPTER VII.

HISTORY.

Lived like an anchorite, and worked like an apostle.

CHANGES fell upon Bolter's Rents, and it
was known to the people of that dismal
region that the proprietary of the court had
changed hands. There are grades of respect-
ability. There were people even in Bolter's
Rents who formed a sort of local gentry by
contrast with their surroundings. To these,
and to all with a remnant of decency, the
alterations insituted by the new proprietor
were matter for almost unmixed congratulation.
But there lurked in that foul den, known to
the police, scores of old criminals and young
ones, burglars, pickpockets, shop-lifters, utterers
of base coin—a terrible tribe. These marau-
ders were all of too low a class in their own
profession to be able to hold their own in it,

and some of their time was spent in the performance of casual honest work. Amongst the more prosperous scoundrels who lived in better lodgings, they were known contemptuously as 'ale-and-porters,' a term used by the British thief to signify people who are occasionally forced by pressure of poverty into honesty's ways. The true professional criminal despises that sort of person, just as an honest mechanic does, and for the same reason —namely, that the person lives in a constant base desertion of principle. The only difference is—though it may be confessed to be considerable—that the mechanic's principle is industry, and the scoundrel's laziness. Now and again, an aristocrat amongst the 'smashers' or the 'cracksmen' hid himself in Bolter's Rents, and was unearthed by the vigilance of the police ; but the predatory creatures who regularly dwelt there were amongst the meanest even of their own mean kind. To them the proceedings of the new proprietor did not seem an unmixed good. A sort of informal official, whom the police were always ready to support, dwelt in the place after its first purification by whitewash ; and all who lived disorderly, were by him despatched to seek a

residence elsewhere. The leaning walls were
straightened by huge hulks of timber—the
broken floors and windows and roofs were all
repaired, and every room was scoured at settled
times. For this, some dozen charwomen who
lived in the court and had hitherto starved were
engaged, and by it they made a plentiful living.
Some of the indwellers fiercely resented the
advent of soap and water and whitewash;
and one hunchbacked hermit of a crossing-
sweeper, who had been born forty years before
in the room he lived in, and had never seen
it scoured in all his life, repelled the intruding
charwoman with his besom, and threatened to
be the death of anybody who laid a scrubbing-
brush upon the time-consecrated filth of his
apartment. Him the informal official grimly
'chucked out' until such time as the ancient
solitary reign of dirty chaos should be mo-
lested. The hunchback bore it better afterwards, though he took an Englishman's privilege, and grumbled, declaring that since
these new ways came in, Bolter's Rents was
no place for a decent man to live in. The
new proprietor, who was a gentleman with
one arm, interviewed this original, and was so
charmed with him, that he gave him half-a-

crown, though he refused to adopt his principles with regard to sanitation.

The new proprietor indeed was in and out of the place all day at first; and was so excessively liberal with his money, that Bolter's Rents rose at him almost to an infant, and begged of him and lied to him with such persistent fluency that he avoided the place afterwards, until the official he had appointed had grubbed out the most poisonous of the human weeds, and little but honest poverty dwelt within the walls of those tumble-down old buildings. Hastings was very tender at first about throwing the thieves adrift. ' Poor beggars !' he said, talking the matter over with the doctor. ' What *can* they do but prey upon society ? If I take your advice, a score of them will be homeless to-morrow. I do not care to be followed by the curses even of such a little drab of a shop-lifter as that we saw this morning. Why not let them stay ?'

' As I am an honest man,' proclaimed the doctor, ' you sicken me. Whoso gives knowing shelter to a criminal, gives countenance to crime, and stands responsible for it in the sight of God and man. If there were no thieves' shelters, there would be no thieves.'

'A good round sentence, doctor,' said Hastings, laughing ; 'but a shaky aphorism.'

'When a man speaks earnestly,' said the doctor, 'he speaks broadly. And the Flippancies—of whom there are too many—take truths broadly stated, put a strained meaning on them, and lightly set them down as lies.'

'I am none of your Flippancies,' responded Hastings. 'I am a Social Reformer, and the proprietor of Bolter's Rents—wherefore let the wise and gentle pity me. Doctor, I pity a scoundrel more than an honest man who is in trouble.'

'Do you ?' said the doctor.

'I do. Because he *is* a scoundrel. Think, doctor, what a terrible thing it is to be a scoundrel by nature. How would you like to be a shop-lifter ? I tell you, sir, the doom of these base thieves is tragic.'

'You are right,' said the doctor. 'Let us go out and form a Thieves' Phalanstery, where pickpockets shall eat turtle and drink Burgundy, and all shall go attired in purple and fine linen, and every man shall have full right to rob his neighbour.'

'When a man speaks earnestly, doctor,' Hastings answered, with a quiet twinkle in his

eyes, 'he speaks broadly. And the Flippancies—of whom there are too many—take
truths broadly stated, and—'

'Go to Bath!' cried the doctor, laughing.

'No,' said Hastings,—'to extremes.'—The
doctor laughed again; and Hastings added,
'You are right; but I have some right on my
side too. It is a pitiful business; and I am
very sorry for the poor wretches, and could
almost find it in my heart to bribe them
into honesty, rather than try to whip them
there.'

'Bribes make no man true!' said the doctor.

'Nor stripes either,' added Hastings.

'They teach at least that first stern and
necessary lesson, Hastings, that the way of
transgressors is hard.'

'Ay!' said Hastings, with more feeling than
he commonly displayed; 'their way is hard.
Poor transgressors!'

These talks did good to each of them, and
advanced the scheme they both had at heart;
and though the doctor often laughed at the
owner of Bolter's Rents, and often with him,
the wildest theories the young gentleman
broached had always a kernel of good sense
and feeling. And the doctor in his turn,

whilst Hastings softened his sterner creed somewhat, bullied the younger man out of most of his extravagances; until between them, with the doctor's wife to lend a helping hand, Bolter's Rents was transformed to an abode of honest and cleanly poverty.

And Hastings had no more effective co-adjutor in all this than his old friend Frank Fairholt, whom he thought he had buried years ago in the Crimea. If one good deed, as Portia sweetly said, shines in this naughty world, as wide as the light which burned at home to welcome her, Frank's blameless life shone like a beacon in the Cimmerian darkness of Bolter's Rents. Had one blackguard dared to insult the quiet, shrinking, broken, ever-helpful man, another blackguard would have been there to knock his fellow-scoundrel down. Though amongst them, not of them, he helped the poverty-stricken, nursed the sick, did a thousand menial gentle offices, was tireless for good, lived like an anchorite, and worked like an apostle. Deep in the ruffian hearts of this abominable crew, his tender and persistent gentleness was cherished in the one honest spot which generations of vice had bequeathed to them. His pitiful

charity fell, like heaven's light and rain, upon
the just and the unjust. He lost two days'
work at one time in nursing a desperado
through an attack of delirium tremens ; and
it is a fact that the man, who was the terror
of the court, got somehow to love his bene-
factor—as a bulldog loves his master, with
a regard which shows itself chiefly by tearing
the master's enemies.

It chanced one night that the statuesque
policeman whom we saw with Hastings a
little while ago, stood posturing with lumpish
grace at the entrance to Bolter's Rents, gazing
with a placid grandeur of demeanour down
Oxford Street. A woman stood a little way
within the entrance with her hands beneath
a tattered apron. Frank came up in the
twilight, and the policeman and the woman
each had to make way for him. The officer
recognised him, and in his curiosity at finding him so far afield from his labours, his
dignity relaxed, and he said, ' Hillo, my good
woming !' in a lordly condescending tone, and
beckoned the woman with a Berlin-gloved
forefinger. ' Do you know the party which
just went down ?' the Peeler queried when
the woman came to him.

' Yes, sir,' said the woman. ' Leastways, he
lives here, as I believe ; but I don't know no
harm agen him.'

' Has he lived here long ? ' the Peeler
asked.

' I've on'y been here three 'ears myself,
sir, the woman answered humbly ; ' but he
was here when I come.'

' Egstrornary ! ' said the officer in reverie.
' He works more than three mile off at the
Docks. They calls him " The Duke " and
" Your Grace," down there.'

' I'm told he's quite the gentleman, sir,'
the woman responded, tremulously grateful
for the official's urbanity.

' They say,' said the policeman, who found
his beat dull, and was glad to unbend—as
a prince, suffering from *ennui*, might care for
once in a way to converse with a ploughman
—'they say as he was wuth 'alf-a-millying
o' money at one time, an' lost it on the
Derby. What's the name he goes by ? '

' Jones, I believe, sir, said the woman re-
spectfully.

' Ah ! ' said the official, scraping his chin
with his thumb and finger—an act in which
the stipendiary magistrate of his own court

looked unusually magisterial—'same party, I make no doubt. Good-night.' The officer swung with majestic even tread along the pavement; and the woman looked after him admiringly, recalling the time when her Joe was just such a fine figure of a man.

And in this wise the fact and the fable about Frank had followed him to Bolter's Rents. All minds, cultivated or vulgar, have a liking for romance; and Frank became after this an embodiment of mystery to many of the people who surrounded him; and some of the women were persuaded that the title by which he was known had once of right belonged to him. Altogether, he was the one remarkable figure in the place; and Hastings heard much of him, and was interested in him. Frank in his turn heard of the new proprietor with a terror and a longing which struggled against each other. Had he lived beyond the extremest span of human years, it is not probable that his horror of his own crime would have perceptibly fallen from that level flood of shame and loathing which had washed his heart ever since his return to London. The storm whose violence had driven those terrible waters over him had died away, and they

were calm now; but he was drowned in a
living death below them. Yet since he had
been so long undiscovered, and had grown so
changed, his fears had learnt to sleep; until
on the night when he was nursing his old
enemy, the friend who had thrown him into
his enemy's hands appeared beside him. Then
they started up, wide - eyed and quivering.
They grew so morbid, that he was afraid
even to run away, lest the act should awake
suspicion. The danger as it seemed to grow
nearer, fascinated him, as some snakes fasci-
nate birds, until it seemed almost to drag him
into Hastings' way. He had wearied Mrs.
Brand's determined efforts to approach him;
for he had never, since the only occasion on
which I have shown them together, so much
as answered her a word, though she had
approached him often. A score of people
whom he had known knew Dr. Brand, and
his unreasoning fears kept him at this distance from her, sorely against his will. His
obstinate silence puzzled her the more, that
she heard continually of his goodness.

'He would only answer me in German,'
Hastings said, when, with the doctor's wife, he
stumbled upon this subject of common interest.

'In German?' asked Mrs. Brand. 'He speaks English beautifully. I don't mean that he speaks English beautifully as a foreigner might, but that he speaks it like an English gentleman. The people call him "The Duke," and are full of stories of his generosity and tenderness. Some of the women have cried to me in talking about him and his kindness.'

'I confess to a share of curiosity in this mystery,' said the doctor from his arm-chair, for it was evening, and his day's work was over. 'I don't place much reliance on that sort of legend; but the people in the Rents are all ready to swear that he had a great fortune and lost it by gambling. If the man is a gentleman, I can understand his reticence. If I were brought down to such a position, I should not be inclined to accept the patronage of any lady or gentleman, however kindly disposed it might be.'

'Nor I either,' said Hastings. 'But if we could get him into co-operation with us, he might help us, and might do himself a great deal of service too. You must allow me to try him, Mrs. Brand.'

'Pray do,' cried the little lady. 'But be

careful not to go too far. He has spoken to
me once only, and then he told me, in a
weary sort of way, which I can't at all de-
scribe or imitate, that he had but one thing
left in the world, and that was his solitude,
and that if I persisted in speaking to him, he
should be driven to leave the place.'

'He hasn't left?' said the doctor briefly.

'No,' said Mrs. Brand; 'but he has never
spoken to me since.'

'I must try him,' said Hastings; and learning, by inquiry at the Rents, when the object
of his search was generally to be found at
home, he sought him on the following Sunday afternoon. The faithful Ali followed his
master up the winding stair; but at a signal
from his hand, remained without the room.
Hastings rapped; and the voice which cried
'Come in,' made his foot pause at the
threshold. The voice awoke no memory,
though it might well have awakened many; but
it brought a strange mood to Hastings—a mood
which most people have known at one time
or another. The time, the darkened stair,
the light within the room, the tawny face
beside him in the shadow, his errand there,
the voice—all seemed familiar to him. He

seemed to know what would meet him within, and what would be said and done, as though this were a re-acting of the doings of a former life, and he remembered just this fragment of it. He entered with this mood upon him.

There sat before him on a rough bench near the window a man who looked past middle age, and yet prematurely old ; by which I mean that you would have said he looked seventy, but could not be more than five-and-fifty. His long hair, which curled inwards at the ends, was silver white ; but the beard which flowed from throat and cheek and chin had still a few jet black hairs in it, and the heavy moustache which drooped above his lips was scarcely grey. The arched black eyebrows marked the face in a singular way, and the pathetic eyes held a most memorable sorrow. All this Hastings had time to notice as he stepped from the shadow into the light. He could not fail to see the look of terror which took the place of sadness in the man's eyes as he advanced, nor could he fail to be surprised at the sudden drooping of the head and the silence, undisturbed except by his laboured breathing, with which the man encountered him.

'Forgive me,' said Hastings, advancing a little further, 'for intruding on you. I am afraid I startled you.' He paused for an answer, but none came. 'Won't you ask me to sit down?' he said a minute later. The lodger, with his chin still crushing his beard against his breast, spoke not a word, but waved his hand towards an unoccupied bench at the far end of the room. Hastings drew the rough seat towards the light, and for a time said nothing, not well knowing what to say. He felt that the silence which confronted him was not sullen, and he was disposed to be patient with the unreasonable fear which made the man shrink away. 'I must ask you not to think that I am intruding,' he said at length, a little disconcerted by the other's passivity. 'The fact is, I bought this place some time ago, and ever since I have been trying to make it decent. You have been working at that task longer than I have, and I want for one thing to thank you for it. You have done good work here — manly work. You've been very kind to these poor beggars, and I am personally obliged to you.'

The lodger's irresponsive silence built a wall about him. He did not move, and only

his breathing, which was agitated and uneven
showed that he was alive. Hastings sat dis-
comfited, regarding him keenly all the time,
and almost gave up his attack already. But
as he looked at the shrinking figure and the
bent head, a pang of sympathy and pity shot
through his heart, and he discerned a tragedy.
The vague tales which were afloat about the
man indicated a surprising folly; but Hastings
was one who had a great deal of sympathy
with a certain sort of fool. So far as the stories
told of his strange tenant might be true, the
follies therein set down were so like the mad-
ness of his own youth, that he could not be
pitiless with them; and the man's charity to
the poor in his own poverty, and his unosten-
tatious and continual patient tending of the
sick, seemed to bespeak a very fine and lovable nature. Under the pressure of this new
feeling, Hastings spoke again.

'You have done much for the cause I have
at heart. Let me do something for you.'—A
motion of the listener's hand waved him back
from that theme in such a fashion as to bring
a blush to his face.—'No,' he said, hurried into
saying more than he had meant to say in the
eagerness of his explanation; 'I am not in-

sulting you by offering charity. I want a quid pro quo. I want to offer you an engagement, which will suit you better than your work at the docks, and be more congenial to you. I want you to act as my almoner amongst the poor here, if you will. I want you to distribute relief among them, and to live with them, as you are doing now. I must find somebody to do the work, and I shall get nobody who knows the people and their wants as you do. They know better than tell lies to you, for you know all about them.'

Frank sat before him motionless and speechless. 'Does he know?' he thought; 'and will he not appear to know? Is this his way of trying to lift me from wretchedness? He knew Tasker. He himself is changed, and I knew *him*. Does he know me? Has he discovered all?' Had he dared, how he could have cast himself before his friend! But there is no space in material nature, though fancy reach from limit to limit of the starry hosts, which can do more than image the gulf which seemed to him to stretch between them.

'Every man,' said Hastings, resolving not to be beaten by this silence, 'has his rights, and one of yours is to order me out of your

place if you want me gone. So long as you
rent this room, it belongs of course to you,
and not to me. You want quiet ; you hate to
be intruded upon. Well, you shall have your
way. I'll tell you what you shall do, if you
like. You shall have a messenger to go between you and Mrs. Brand, and none of us
will trouble you. I'll get some furniture sent
in here, and make you a little more comfortable ; and you shall just go about among the
people and see to them, and do what you can
for them. If any of them cannot possibly pay
their rent, your statement shall be a sufficient
acquittance of their liability ; and if any de-
serving person is in want of food or medicine,
or fire or clothes, you shall get what is wanted
at my charges ; but you must be down like a
hammer on idleness and pretence. You shall
set all your expenses down ; and Mrs. Brand
will see that the money has been properly
expended. That will be only fair to you, of
course, and will be quite proper and business-
like into the bargain. Now, what do you
say ? '

He said nothing. He listened to the tones
of his old friend ; and though the flippancy
which had marked them once had vanished

altogether, he knew that he could have sworn
to the voice with absolute certainty, and he
would not trust his own even with a word,
lest it should betray him. He was not sure
of the truth, but he was almost sure, and Hope
came hand in hand with belief to persuade him
that he was not recognised.

'If you do not care to give me an answer
now,' Hastings went on with a gentle patience
which surprised his listener, 'you can send me
word when you like. Or I will call fôr your
decision this day week. That shall be the
arrangement. If you do not send to me before
Sunday next, I will come here for your answer.
Good afternoon.'

Still no answer came ; and with a repetition
of his farewell, Hastings left the garret ; and
the faithful Ali came out of his dusky corner
and followed him down-stairs into the street,
and home. Frank was greatly shaken by the
interview. Whilst Hastings spoke, his own
struggling griefs and longings took him by the
throat so strongly, that the force by which he
held his peace and made no sign exhausted
him, and he sat trembling with hysteric tears
after his friend's departure. He thought of
the proposal Hastings had made, and his own

way seemed clear to him. Whatever declared itself as duty, *that* must he do, and no other, until it should be done and life should be over. The way was open to him; and before the end of the week came he spoke to· Penkridge.

'Go to the landlord, and tell him from me that I will undertake the work he offers. Tell him I shall have time enough to see to it all when my work at the docks is over. Tell him also that I only undertake it on this condition—that I am left alone. If any attempt is made to intrude upon my quiet, I will go away.'

Penkridge, who had little enough good left in him, had at least some sentiment of gratitude, and Frank had done so much for him, that he was his willing servant. He delivered the message; and Hastings sent back word that his strange tenant's wishes should be respected. There grew up in Bolter's Rents a power for good which worked amazingly. The almoner of the rich man's bounty had a heart and hand for it, and his charities were done charitably. Many forlorn hearts heard their first word of human comfort from Frank's ·ips, and the gladness he brought to others was reflected back upon himself. And although his burden was one which must needs be borne until the restful breast of Mother Earth closed over it and him, he grew slowly to a strength which was equal to his day, and Peace dwelt with him, mournful-eyed.

CHAPTER VIII.

AUTOBIOGRAPHY.

*The preacher poured forth an impetuous torrent of
self-accusation.*

'TO be well in chambers,' Thackeray writes
in that novel of his which has always
been my favourite, 'is melancholy and lonely
and selfish enough ; but to be ill in chambers
—to pass nights of pain and watchfulness—
to long for the morning and the laundress—
to serve yourself your own medicine by your
own watch—to have no other companion for
long hours but your own sickening fancies
and fevered thoughts : no kind hand to give
you drink if you are thirsty, or to smooth
the hot pillow that crumples under you—
this indeed is a fate so dismal and tragic,
that we shall not enlarge upon its horrors,
and shall only heartily pity those bachelors

in the Temple who brave it every day.'
All this I suffered; and I made myself
worse by the rebellion in which I raged
against my Uncle Ben's suspicion. I learned
afterwards that three days after my seizure,
Gregory, who had paid several visits to
my rooms, and had succeeded in making
no one hear his summons at the door, way-
laid the laundress in his anxiety about me;
and finding the state I was in, rushed boldly
after Dr. Brand, and told him not only the
fact of my illness, but the reason of it. The
good doctor attended me, and sent a prac-
tised nurse, who superseded the laundress;
and having discovered her in a state of in-
toxication, with a bottle of my brandy on
the table before her, took upon herself to
discharge that faithless functionary, who re-
venged herself by pitying statements to the
other men whose chambers she attended, as
to the sorrow she felt at seeing such a nice
young gentleman take to drink so early. The
doctor's medicine and the nurse's tending
brought me round; and for some days after
the fever had left me, I lay quite tranquil
and at rest; but my after-recovery was made
slow by the misery of mind which I endured.

I came out of my sick-room aged and altered. The Holborn lawyer had no comfort for me when I called upon him, though his manner was distinctly sympathetic and gentle. He offered to pay me at any time the first portion of the allowance my uncle had proposed to make me; but I refused it sullenly, and told him that until Mr. Hartley had withdrawn his accusation, I would hold no dealings with him, and would never more accept a farthing at his hands.

'How do you propose to live?' Mr. Bilton asked me. 'You have no profession as yet.'

'I do not know,' I answered, with a bitter and resentful sense of the injustice which had been done me. 'No man with a pair of hands need starve.' He shook his head at that with a pitying smile, which, in the soreness of my heart, I received almost as if it had been a blow.

'When you change your mind,' he answered, 'you can come to me.'

'My mind will not change on that matter,' I responded. 'Let me know if you learn anything from the police.'

He promised me that; and I left him, and went back to my rooms, to survey the prospect which spread itself before me. It looked very barren ; and I was groaning in spirit over it, and was lashing myself into a great state of rage against Uncle Ben, as the author of my misery, when Gregory came in.

'Jack,' he said, with a friendly hand upon my shoulder, 'what do you propose to do?'

'I don't know,' I answered fretfully. 'I think I shall sell off the things, send the proceeds to Bilton, for my uncle, and enlist.'— He kept his hand upon my shoulder whilst I spoke, and gave me a little pull at the last word, which indicated a decided negative.— 'What else can I do?' I asked him gloomily.

'It is quite clear,' said Gregory, 'that you can't receive any more money from your uncle until this cloud between you disappears.'

'I will never take another penny from him,' I cried hotly. 'And if any chance present itself, I will pay back every penny he has spent upon me, though I have to pay it to his grandchildren.'

'You can't do that on a shilling a day, you duffer,' said Gregory, with his hand still upon my shoulder. 'Do you know what I do for a living?'

'I didn't know,' I answered, 'that you did anything. I thought your father made you an allowance.'

'My father's money,' he said gravely, 'has been sunk in mines, and swallowed in the Gulf of Mexico, and strewn broadcast over the tracts of Patagonia, and invested in the great vineyard speculation in Smith's Sound, and dissipated generally on hopeful experiments which bade fair to yield a rich profit —to the promoters. I suppose the promoters have profited by them; but his children have been keeping him this past two years, and he hasn't one financial feather left to fly with. I don't blame him,' said Gregory, making a curious grimace. 'He meant well. He never cared for money, or understood it; but he thought it would be nice to leave us all millionaires, and in the attempt to do it he ruined himself. That's all. Now, how do you think I live?'

'How do you live?'

'By teaching my grandmother the art and mystery of egg-sucking,' he answered. 'I am a public instructor. I have this morning completed an article on "Sugar" for the new Encyclopædia. I did one on "Soap" last

week. I am the author of that instructive
volume *The World's Workshops.* I write
for reviews, magazines, newspapers. A farce
of mine will be played next week at the Olym-
pic. You must come and see it. I am writing a novel for a firm in Manchester, who
will publish it simultaneously in thirteen
provincial weekly journals. "The pen is
mightier than the sword," as the Dandy of
Literature most truly saith. You can only
earn a bob a day with the sabre. I make
six hundred a year with the quill, and hope to
make more in time. All is fish that comes
to my net. I shall be in Parliament next
session—not as a member, but as a salaried
censor of the House, a leader-writer to a
· daily journal. I have been at this work now
for four years, and I am doing well at it.
Now this brings me to my question again.
You must earn a living somehow, and you
must do it like a gentleman. Why not try
my plan ?'

I flushed at the suggestion. Of all the
fairy palaces I had built in fancy for myself
to live in—and they had been many in my
hopeful days — none had seemed so well
worth living for as that in which Hope en-

shrined certain literary works of mine, as yet unwritten.

'But who would pay for any work that I could do?' I asked. 'I am untried. I—I— *think—*'

'Oh, yes,' cried Gregory, 'you think! I know you think. Put your thoughts on paper. Look here, Jack, I can give you a chance. This is a secret, mind you, and it must be kept.' I nodded 'Of course ;' and he went on : 'Lord Chesterwood is aiming at a place in the ministry, and he is establishing a daily journal. Stone will be editor. He leaves the *Daily Mail* on purpose to rule over us. I am parliamentary leader-writer. You shall be "Our Special Commissioner," if you will, and you shall hit on a theme at once and write a series of articles. Let me give you a hint. Suppose you take the London Slums, which have been "done" again and again, and *will* be "done" again and again, so long as they and newspaper writers live side by side. Attempt no fine writing. Be as accurate, as uncompromising as a photograph. Make your sentences short and curt, and let each sentence petrify a fact. Keep your eyes open, and set down everything you see.

Don't be afraid of being commonplace or vulgar, but be rigidly and strictly true. Use no too-powerful adjectives. There is nothing simpler than the style I mean, and nothing that takes better with the public, which is made up of matter-of-fact people for the most part, and doesn't care for high-falutin'. '

I asked with some misgiving if Gregory had influence enough to secure this work for me.

'Yes,' he answered ; ' if you only do these first things decently. Set about them at once. We shall be ready to begin in a month, and you must start with us. I have named you to Stone already—promising, brilliant young fellow, did well at college, nephew of Hartley, the great millionaire, anxious to join literary guild, win his spurs, that sort of thing.'

'Why did you speak of my uncle ?' I asked gloomily.

'He *is* your uncle, isn't he ?' said Gregory. ' Very well ; I said he was.'

'He must know,' I said, 'that my uncle and I are parted, and that I have no hopes from him. I will not sail under false colours.'

'You Quixotic young idiot,' said Gregory, with rough amity ; ' don't talk Rot. What's Hecuba to him—meaning your estimable uncle

—or he to Hecuba ? You set to work on
your articles. Think of a title, crisp, allitera-
tive if possible, and accurately descriptive.
Let me see the first, and I'll tell you if it'll
do. You'll find me a cruel critic ; so take
care.'

I had at that time thirty pounds in hand,
and half of that had to go in payment of a
quarter's rental for my chambers; but I looked
forward with new hope now, and under Æsop's
directions, I went to work at once, to make
this small sum a little larger. The following
night saw me in Whitechapel, in company with
an inspector and a sergeant of police ; and
in a week I was fully acquainted with the
locale of the slums, and knew something of
their characteristics. Every night when I
came home, I wrote the story of the evening's adventures in complete detail ; and every
morning after, I trimmed and polished with
zealous care. Then I gave a week to the
complete rewriting of the series, and began
to regard it as a masterpiece of literary effort.
My note to Gregory, in which I announced
that they were ready for inspection, was written
modestly enough ; but I felt within myself
that the articles would stagger him more than

a little. When he came to read them, I had
arrived at the belief that they were filled with
perhaps the vilest trash which had ever been
put upon paper; and when he took them away
with the simple statement that he thought they
would do, I felt immensely relieved. By-and-
by there came to me by post a bundle of
damp strips of paper in which the articles
appeared in type; and though I knew them
by heart already, I read them through and
through with an ever-increasing pride and joy,
and resolved that they would take the town
by storm. At last the paper appeared; and
on the placard of contents I with my own
eyes beheld in the public streets the printed
title of my series. The Strand waltzed with
me. I paid a penny for a copy of the new
journal, and wondered if the boy who served
me knew that there was an article of mine in
it, and what he would think if he did know
it. I opened and folded back the paper, and
read the article anew as I walked to my chambers. If all the hurrying crowds that went
between Charing Cross and Clement's Danes
had formed in rows to see me pass, and had
cheered me as if I had been a royal procession on a gala-day, I could not have felt

prouder.   Every placard on the walls from
which the words my pen had written looked
upon me, was a tribute to me; and when at
last a long file of sandwichmen came along
the street, each bearing at back and front an
invitation to the general public to purchase
the new journal and to read my articles, spe-
cially mentioned in large type, I was almost
beside myself, and was glad to walk into the
quiet of the inn, lest my emotion should be
observed.   The upshot of the business was
that I received a cheque for the series, and
that I was engaged at a settled weekly salary
as a descriptive writer on the new daily journal.   The salary I received opened no visions
of El Dorado to my gaze; but it was enough
to live on quietly.   I dropped out of my
place in the hospital; and nobody there, except Dr. Brand, knew why.   But the crowd
of friends who had sought the society of the
acknowledged nephew of the great millionaire,
dropped off when the great millionaire's supply had ceased to gild me; and I knew on
whose help and friendship I could rely.

In all the devious ways in which my life
has been guided, I can but recognise a Master
Hand.   I have been moved inexorably here

and there, against my will, apart from my will. The plan of my life has no more been mine than the words written by my pen this moment are dictated by it. And now in the halting-place of life at which I tell this story, I can see the plan which my unwilling movements here and there have traced, and I know that I was guided to a settled end.

My articles did not take the town by storm ; but they attracted at least the notice of the editor, who made up his mind from them that the low life of London was my especial track. He kept me on it. He found for me series after series, until at last he set me upon the great religious revival, which at that time was agitating the lower classes of London ; and I followed the course of this strange tide into such curves and hollows of the human shore as I could reach. On a certain night, when the rain was falling dismally, I crossed the river afoot, and walked towards a great wooden tabernacle in which the chief services of the revival were held. It was Sunday, and the streets were blank. I remember the look of the flickering gaslights in the dusk—the grimy perspective of the mean houses as they stretched out towards the dark in dreary

monotony of ugliness — the sullen pools of
rain in the breaches of the pavement—the
chill discomfort of the fretful wind. When I
reached the place, I was a little surprised to
find that the service had begun ; but a glance
at the bills upon the wooden walls showed me
that I had mistaken the announced time by
half-an-hour.   It mattered little ; and I entered
finding even standing-room with difficulty.   A
man upon the platform was frenzying himself
in prayer, and the vast crowd followed his
appeals with cries and groans.   When the
prayer was over, another man gave out a
hymn, and eight thousand voices rolled it to
the roof.   I have heard nothing like that rough
singing elsewhere.   The hymn over, a third
man offered prayer ; and then, with first a
rustle and a curious swaying in the crowd,
and then a dead silence, the congregation
settled itself to hear the sermon.   A tall
figure, clad in black, came forward to the
platform's edge.   The light was dim, and
there was a positive cloud of steam from
the damp clothes of the crowd ; but I seemed
to know the poise of that golden head,
and the slow imperious motion of the arm
by which the preacher commanded silence.

And with the first tones of his voice, I knew
him. It was Gascoigne. At first, I was so
amazed to see him there that I could scarcely
find a thought for what he said ; but remembering that more than one clergyman of the
Church of England had given countenance
to this movement, though none, so far as I
knew, had spoken from the platform, I composed myself to listen. If such a sermon as
he preached had been written, few men of
taste could have approved it. Had it been
delivered in a church and to a cultivated
audience, its force would have been lost. But
Gascoigne, as I knew now, was an orator, and
somehow he knew his people, and he swayed
the crowd with the passion and the pathos
of his words. Every simile was trite. There
was nothing beyond the comprehension of the
meanest ; but everything was dramatic, and
instinct with a fire that set even my veins
tingling, though I was bent rather on criti-
cism than devotion. And his voice was wonderful to hear. It rang over us like a clarion ;
it moved us like a wind ; it rose to height
beyond height of passionate denunciation. It
fell to dead silence for a moment, and then
its rare music took a softer mood ; and in a

while it passed to exultation, and rose again majestic, and thrilled and awed and melted the rough souls that heard it. But if I had been amazed before, astonishment transcended itself when the preacher poured forth an impetuous torrent of self-accusation. He, vilest among sinners, he, most faithless to the truth, must yet preach, for the hand of God was upon him. So he spoke; and the strange discourse continued with an appeal to the Divine Mercy, which was echoed in sobs and prayers about the place, and closed amidst a storm of tears and cries. I made an effort to struggle through the crowd towards the platform; but the stream was all against me —crawling slowly to the front door, and when I had resigned my effort, and had made a way round the building to the preacher's retiring-room, it was dark and empty. I went home in a condition of uneasy wonder, with a fear about Gascoigne in my thoughts which no reasoning in his favour could altogether stifle.

He had never been a good correspondent; and of late years, our letters, though full of heartiness, were brief and rare on both sides. That had never made a difference in my friendship to him, or indicated any, as I believed, on either side. I had written to him once concerning my Uncle Ben's suspicion of me, and had received a letter of sympathy and indignant protest ; but my later letters setting forth my new prospects had not been answered. I began to ask myself if Gascoigne had thrown away his prospects in the Church ; but I could resolve on no belief, and was left—as I have said already—in uneasy wonder. On the following night I went again through the wintry rain to the Tabernacle, and reaching the place early, took advantage of my occupation as a journalist, and secured a seat in front. Gascoigne did not appear ; but I learned on inquiry that he was to preach on Wednesday. I cannot tell by what instinct I did it ; but on that night I waived my privilege, and took a place some twenty rows down in the middle of the central division. When the doors were opened for the admission of the populace, men and women stormed into the building headlong and fought for places. The aisles were choked, and the whole place was crammed almost to suffocation. After a long pause, a sudden swaying in the aisles, and a sudden cessation of the coughing sounds which had hitherto filled the building, sent my eyes to the platform, and I saw, amid the half-dozen square-set, white-tied, bullet-headed men who took their places on it, the tall form and the golden hair of my friend. From where I sat I could see him clearly. Even his lips were pallid, but his eyes were ablaze with the fire of an intense excitement. After one keen glance, which seemed to take in all the faces in the crowd but mine, he bent his head, and through all the preliminary service his eyes were fixed upon the floor. Once or twice he raised his hand to his forehead, and I could see a little tremor in it, which told clearly how high his nerves were strung. The service over, he arose and gave out his text, and waiting until the rustle of leaves with which many of the congregation confirmed his citation of the words, was ended, he began to speak, at first slowly and with labour, each syllable falling distinct and clear in spite of the agitation which shook him. In a minute that agitation had left him, and he was master of himself, and thenceforth master of the crowd. I watched him intently—my glance was fastened to his face, but he never looked at me until he seemed to approach the end

of his discourse. Clean in the middle of a
word, some mortal-seeming pain struck him
at the very instant when his eyes met mine.
His face grew on a sudden deathly in its
pallor, and a terrible hush struck over the
place. Both his hands went to his heart for
a moment, and then he cast out his arms and
threw his head backward like a swimmer in
heavy waters who gives up the struggle.
'Gascoigne!' A cry tore the air. Was it
mine? I scarcely knew whether it were mine
or no; but it rang wildly in my ears as I
rushed—how I cannot tell—towards the platform. He was down. He had measured his
length upon the floor, and mine were the first
arms about him. I could do nothing but hold
up his head and look round in an imploring
agony; but there were steadier hands and
better nerves than mine about him. The
crowd began to storm the platform, and I
can dimly remember that a burly man with a
loud commanding voice ordered the people to
stand aloof and wait. As we bore the limp
figure to the retiring-room, one followed busy
at the cravat which bound Gascoigne's throat;
and when it was loosened, the head rolled
back so lifelessly, that I turned sick "``'

horror at the thought that he was dead. He was not dead; but he had swooned, and he had fallen heavily, and his head was injured. When his pale eyelids raised themselves at last, and his ghostly eyes met mine, he turned with a faint moan and a shudder of the limbs, and his eyes closed again. But after a time, he sat up with my arms about him.

'What was it, brother?' one of the busiest of the helpers asked, as Gascoigne looked round with troubled ghostly eyes and faint quick breathing.

'The heart,' he answered, feebly striking his breast with his left hand, 'pierced—by a pain—like a knife.'

Some one had bound a white handkerchief, dipped first in water, about his head, and there were a few drops of blood upon it. His face was touched with blood also, and the water-spots hung upon his lashes like tears.

'Will some one be good enough to call a four-wheeler?' I asked, gathering a little courage. 'You will come home to my chambers?' I said to Gascoigne; and he answered with a tremor which alarmed me anew.

'Yes, I will—come.' Then feebly wandering round with those ghostly eyes among the troubled and sympathetic faces which surrounded him, he said brokenly, ' It is—the hand—of God.'

'Ay, brother,' said the man who had just spoken. 'Cling to that.'

Gascoigne could only moan in answer. His eyes closed again; and once more I felt a swift shudder run through him as he lay in my arms.

After what seemed to be a long pause, a cab was brought; and Gascoigne, supported on each side, walked down the broken way which ran by the wooden structure. The builders had left it full of hollows and ends of timber, and we went stumbling about in the dark with the sick man between us until we reached the road. There we helped Gascoigne into the vehicle; and I, taking a seat beside him, bade the cabman drive to Clement's Inn. When we reached Waterloo Bridge, and the cab paused whilst I paid the tollman, Gascoigne laid his hand upon my arm, and called me by name. I begged him to rest; and he lay back murmuring to himself, but made no further effort to address me. When we reached the gates, I gave him my arm; and the cabman helping him on the other side, we went slowly to my chambers, and set him in an arm-chair there. When I dismissed the cabman, I gave Gascoigne a glass of brandy; and the room being chill and dismal-looking, I put a light to the fire, which soon began to burn up cheerfully. I drew off his boots, though he made what seemed a fretful effort to oppose me, and brought him slippers, and he sat sipping his brandy-and-water and gazing at the fire.

'Jack,' he said suddenly in an excited voice, 'I will tell you everything. I will make a clean breast of it; and then what *will* come *may* come.'

I could see a feverish light in his eyes, and I noticed, too, that his complexion changed rapidly from red to white and back again.

'You shall tell me what you will to-morrow, I answered; 'but you shall tell me nothing now. You are not fit to talk. You shall sit here quietly, and I will fetch a doctor.'

'No,' he said excitedly; 'I need no doctor. I can tell what ails me without a doctor. There is only one cure in the universe, and I have it in my hands. Listen to me!'

'You shall not hurt yourself by talking now,'

I said, beginning to fear that his mind was affected by the excitement of the night and the sudden illness which had attacked him. 'If you will not have a doctor, I shall insist upon your going to bed. Come now; let me help you.'

He submitted, but with a chafing restlessness. He was so weak, and his mood so variable, that when he was at last in bed, and I laid my hand upon his shoulder in bidding him good-night, he broke into hysterical sobs, and I had hard work to calm him. Thinking he would be more likely to sleep if alone, I left him, and sat beside the fire thinking and smoking. I looked in upon him once or twice; and at length finding that his slumbers, at first feverish and broken, had grown settled, I ventured to go to bed myself. I lay awake for a long time, and could hear his regular breathing from the other room; but at last sleep overpowered me.

I awoke in the morning with a sense of trouble, which resolved itself into a remembrance of Gascoigne's sudden illness. Slipping out of bed, I opened the door of his room noiselessly and looked in. To my surprise, I found that he had left his bed; and I became alarmed when a visit to the sitting-room assured me that he had quitted my chambers.

CHAPTER IX.

HISTORY.

*' I am glad you have a good heart; I hope you will
be happy.'*

I T came to pass after many years had
gone thus heavily by, that Frank felt
in his heart a great yearning for green fields;
and it came into his mind that he was
not much longer for the world. And the
yearning drew him day by day, until he had
no power to hold himself against it; so he
made ready for a journey, and set out in the
autumn-time, when the harvest was yellowing
towards the sickle, and the fruits were ripen-
ing on the trees. He had been more than
sixteen years a prisoner in the town, and the
solemn sad delight of the fields and woods
filled him with awe, and with new longing
towards the grave. He went bowed with his
crime and his repentance and the weight of

the slow years ; and the rural people whom
he met looked with surprise at his sorrowful
face and his silver beard and his heavy long-
shore dress ; but somehow, for the dignity
that was upon him, forbore to mob him.

He went, as though an invisible chain had
drawn him, in the direction of his old home.
Even the most morbid cowardice may feel
secure after years of escape, and Frank's
dread had given way to a certainty that he
need fear no recognition. Yet when he came
to Hetherton, he trembled a little inwardly
as he walked the main street and saw Mr.
Crisp at the bank door talking with a friend.
The place was greatly altered ; but the bank
was unchanged ; and neither the corn-chandler
nor the baker had invested as yet in plate-
glass windows. But there were new shops
and new names ; and he had no more of
friendly greeting at heart for the old town
than it had of welcome for his coming. He
felt it alien and foreign, and the few familiar
things left reproached him.

But when once he had skirted the new and
raw-looking houses which made a cheerless
fringe to the town, and seemed an appanage
altogether ill suited to it, the fields gave his

tired soul a melancholy welcome. He had climbed that great oak as a lad, and its mighty arms and luxuriant foliage were pictured on the first canvas he had sold. Red tiles of a little cottage, blue smoke from the hearth, the deep green of foliage with a leaf sienna-coloured here and there, and here and there a flash of red and yellow like a flame—this was the scene which had made his first successful picture, and had been painted at this season a score of years ago or more. He could almost see under the hedges amid the quaker grasses and the ferns the children who were nutting there in his picture. There was a gap in the distant belt of foliage before the landscape faded to the hill and mingled with the tints of the softly-clouded skies, and he could remember the shape the departed trees had taken. Half a mile farther was a meadow in which his brother Will and he had fought in boyhood; and Frank remembered that he had won, though he had the wrong side in the quarrel. There was scarcely a field that had not its memories for him; and here at last was the entrance to the lane in which he had persuaded his brother to lend him his name for the last time. That lane

led nowhere save to his father's house, and
he was full of fears as he set foot in it.   But
the longing which drew him on was not to
be resisted, and he went with slow steps,
reluctant and yet eager.   Did his father live?
he asked himself, or was the old house given
over to his brother? or had even his brother
vanished with the years?   The place might
be in the hands of strangers.   Who could tell
in such a lapse of time what had happened?
He heard a step in the rustling leaves beyond
a bend in the lane, and stood uncertain whether
to retreat or to advance.   He longed for a
familiar form, and dreaded it; but the foot-
step coming nearer, brought only a groom in
sight.   The man regarded him curiously but
spoke civilly enough.

'Did you want anything up at the house?'

'No,' Frank answered, shaking his head;
'nothing.'

'This road don't led nowhere else,' said the
groom.

'I know,' said Frank.

'You don't belong about here, do you?'
asked the groom.

'I knew the place forty years ago, Frank answered.   'Does the old family still live here?'

'Yes,' said the groom; 'Squire Fairholt lives here.'

Is the old Squire alive?' Frank asked with outward calm, but inward misgiving.

'Ah!' said the groom, a little ungraciously; '*he's* alive, right enough.'

Frank, with a farewell motion of the head, was passing on, when the groom added warningly, 'This is a private road, you know.'

'I know,' Frank answered again. 'But I want to see the old place. That is all.'

'Well, there ain't no harm in that, as fur as *I* see,' the groom responded. 'Only, don't let the Squire see you. If he does, he won't leave you nose enough to swear by—that's all. Good-morning.'

'Good - morning,' Frank responded, and passed on whilst the groom stood to look after him. He reached the gates which opened on the drive, and saw through a gap in the hedge behind which he ensconced himself, the figure of an old man, who walked to and fro on the gravel. He knew the old man for his father, and his heart yearned over him with indescribable love and sorrow. Whilst he watched with tear-dimmed eyes, there came another figure to join that upon the walk—a portly gentleman of middle age, with square shoulders and a brown beard; and after he had watched a while, the outcast knew him for his brother. He could hear the murmur of their talk, though only a disconnected word reached him, with no meaning, now and then; and he turned away.

'They have buried me years ago,' he thought, 'with my disgraces.' He strove to be calm; but the regrets and loves and yearnings which wrestled in his heart overcame him before he had left the lane, and he sat down on the bank and struggled to recover his composure. Whilst he sat thus, fighting down the passions which fought within, another step came rustling through the dead leaves, and looking up, he saw a face which almost brought him to his knees. For it seemed to him that his mother was before him; but the wild thought lasted only for a flash of time; and though he had not seen her since she left infancy, his heart told him that this was his sister. Her glance met his with pitying inquiry.

'Are you ill, or in pain?' she asked.

'No,' he answered gently; and arose and stood before her without fear. She at least could have no knowledge of him—no remembrance.

'But you were crying,' she said simply. 'Are you in trouble ? Do you want anything at the Hall ? '

'I was born near here,' he answered, looking upon her with a sad and tender pleasure ; 'and I have not seen the place for many years.'

'You have been abroad ? ' she asked, gazing with frank and unfearing interest in his eyes.

'No,' he answered. 'But I have been many, many years away.' He looked older than his father, and she took him to mean fifty or sixty years.

'And are your friends all gone ? '

'I am alone,' he said, not mournfully, for he thought rather of the sweet face and pitying eyes than of his own condition.

'That is very sad,' she said. Do you—' She stopped short with a little blush ; and he, seeing that she had drawn forth her purse, waved his hand against it with a melancholy smile.

'No,' he said gently ; 'but I am glad that you have a good heart; I hope you will be happy.' Then seeing that she scarcely knew what response to make, and that she surveyed

him with a little trouble in her eyes, he bared
his head and bowed to her, and stood on one
side to let her pass.   But she lingered still.
She was the Queen of all the country-people,
and her fearless candid nature shone out in her
lovely eyes and her beautiful imperious face,
which was stately and yet tender.

'You do not speak like one of the country-
people,' she said, as he stood bareheaded
before her.   A look of wonder and inquiry
crossed her face, a glance almost of recognition,
lost in perplexity.   It alarmed him, and he
cast his eyes upon the ground and bent his
head.

'I have spent my life in London,' he answered.   'Good-day, madam.'   For a second
she lingered ; but there was something in the
figure and face before her which forbade the
cross-examination with which she would have
assailed any of the village people.   Her answer included an involuntary 'Sir,' at which
she crushed her lips a second later, fearing
that it might have sounded like a satire.   It
was not until she had left him far behind that
she asked herself what it was in the stranger
which had made her answer him so.   'It was
no wonder,' she said then, 'for he took off that

old hat like a nobleman.' She thought of his voice, and could almost rehear its words : ' I am glad that you have a good heart ; I hope you will be happy.' The approval of the shabbily dressed, picturesque, strange old man, though it seemed familiar, did not offend her. ' He is like somebody,' she thought, pleasantly interested ; ' or perhaps he is like a picture I have seen. A head of Rembrandt's ? I am sure he has been a gentleman. Only a gentleman could speak as he did.' And she went away, weaving romances about him—mere cobwebs of invention to catch flies of fancy. ' I should like to know all about him,' she said to herself, little guessing how happy her ignorance kept her.

Frank watched her tall and graceful figure out of sight, losing it now and again in the dimness of his eyes. Then he journeyed into the main road, and walked until the well-remembered walls of Hartley Hall appeared. He did not pass by the great gates, but took a by-road which led him to the village through the corn-fields, where many a shock of corn stood ready for the wain. Emerging upon the high-road, he was aware of a great arch of evergreens at which workmen were still busy.

A man on a scaffolding was nailing over the foliage of the arch a linen scroll on which in scarlet baize were marked the words, ' May their Union be Happy.' There were flags everywhere in the village street; and there were two other arches visible in the distance. The village people were looking on at the completion of the display; the butcher with his hat at the back of his head, and his hands tucked beneath a white apron; the landlord of *The King God Bless Him*, at the door of that loyally-named hostel, with a pint jug in one hand and a yard of clean clay in the other, blinking comfortably in the afternoon sunshine; the local constable in official cap and trousers, but unofficial coat; the grocer in his snowy shirt-sleeves, with a quill behind his ear; the curate directing the proceedings of the decorators; many children; two or three old women in blue or scarlet cloaks; and one old man in a smock-frock. A pleasant rural picture in the autumn sunshine. Frank saw that it indicated the approaching marriage of some local magnate, but took no great interest in the matter, being filled with his own thoughts. He was thinking chiefly how much less burdensome it would be to spend his last days in the quiet of

the country, than amidst the din of town. He
would rather that his grave were green, and
that the sun should shine upon it sometimes.
But he knew, in spite of his desire, that duty
held him to Bolter's Rents. He had found a
work there ; and he could but know, if he were
never so humble in his thoughts, that there
were some there who could ill spare him. ' I
will rest here to-night,' he said to himself, ' and
to-morrow I will go back to London. He
entered the common room of the little inn and
called for a humble meal.

' Theer ull be rar' doin's yer, in the mornin','
said the landlord, as he set the brown loaf and
the cheese before his guest, and flanked them
with a cup of thin cider.

' Ay ? ' said Frank but little interested.

' Ay indeed,' said the landlord. ' Theer
won't a-be such a thing again for many a'ear,
and theer ain't a-been nothin' like it, not in *my*
time afore.'

' What is it to be ? ' Frank asked, being civil
by nature with all sorts and conditions of
men.

' Did you ever yeer o' Mr. Hartley ? ' asked
the landlord. ' Well, his niece do be a-goin to
be married to-morrow.'

'Mr. Hartley of Hartley Hall?' said Frank, feeling his heart beat like a sledge-hammer.

'That's him,' said the landlord. 'Her's a-goin' to be married to young Squire Fairholt up to the Hall theer—Island Hall, up Wrethe-dale-way, like.'

'I know the place,' said Frank, controlling himself to quiet speech.

'They do say,' the landlord went on, 'as her an' young Squire's brother used to be very thick together in bygone times. But I doan't know naught about that, for I warn't settled yer not till later. They be both middle-aged; but they do seem to ha' struck up a match at last. Young Squire 'll be main rich now, um do say. Be you a foreigner?'

'I have not been here for a long time,' Frank answered.

'Ah!' said the landlord; 'it doan't much matter. Anybody 'll be welcome up at the new Hall to-morrer. Theer 'ud be enough *an'* to spare, if the country-side was to come in. Theer's three sheep and a ox a-goin' fur to be roasted, whole. An' Squire Hartley he ain't the man to be sparin' with the poor, that I ull say. He ain't like one o' th' old gentry, as they talks about sometimes, as is as poor as poor, an' as proud as proud. I doan't hold along o' they,' said the landlord, who, in spite of the loyalty of his sign, may have been something of a republican.

Frank answered his further talk as well as he was able ; and when at last the innkeeper went away to the door and resumed his watching of the final decorations of the triumphal arch, he noticed that the guest stayed an unusual time above the bread and cheese, and went back, on pretence of having something to do in the room, to see what was happening to the provisions. He saw that there was little to fear on that head, but cleared away to prevent the chance of mischief. Frank had drawn back from the table, and was sunk fathoms deep in memory's waters. He was trying to divine whether or not Will had long cared for Maud ; and he came at length to see that Will had always cared for her. 'Why so patient ? Why so patient ?' he murmured. Perhaps Maud had only now yielded ; and yet one negative in such a matter would have been enough for Will. Could he trust himself to see them go by to-morrow ? Yes ; he would trust himself. He would see Maud once more ; and she should have his prayers

at least, though she would never know it.
'All these years,' he muttered in his beard,
thinking of the changes which time might have
made in her, and questioning, should he know
her face ? He strayed about the village fields
till nightfall, and then went back to the little
inn, and was shown to a low-pitched bedroom with clean walls of carved oak whitewashed,—after the manner of British rusticity
dealing with carved oak.   There were two
beds in the room ; and a lanky lad who was
a sort of factotum to the inn, would sleep in
in one of them.   Frank sat awhile on the bedside, looking out at the open widow, round
which the ivy talked in leafy whispers.   The
night was warm and silent, and the voices
from the taproom went far afield on the still
air.   All the talk was of the morrow's festivities
—of the ox and the three sheep and the
limitless ocean of beer.   One by one the
people below took leave, and their voices
died away on the wide-spread tranquillity of
the harvest-field.   The moon, as yet a sickle,
hung steadfast in the violet of the lower skies,
with one keen star for a companion.   A sound
of clanging bars and grating bolts warned
him that the house was being closed ; and

he went to bed before his room-companion
came up, and lay still, looking at the sharp
outlines of the leaves against the fathom-
less clear dusk of the heaven, with here
and there the crisp light of a star in it. No
sleep visited him ; but he lay wan and worn
in the darkness, and arose ghostlike with
the dawn, and awaited the coming of the
wedding cortège. Straying along the highway, he silently noted all the preparations.
Here was a stand from which the school
children would sing a hymn. A carpenter
was putting the finishing touches to it ; and
Frank stood to watch, not guessing that he
had lain ill of fever under this man's roof.
The carpenter, with his lips full of nails, gave
the onlooker a muffled good-morning, not guessing that the one great tragedy on which his life
had edged, stood now in bodily form before
him. The time passed, and the sound of
bells came over the woods and the cornfields
—a merry peal. They had rung for Maud
in his dream years ago, and now their sound
drew him as his longing for the fields and
for home had drawn him ; and his footsteps,
eager yet reluctant, took him to the church.
The bells were silent ; but there was a

voice within the church. He had reached the
churchyard from the fields, for he knew every
foot of the country; and looking over the
close-trimmed hedge that bounded it, he saw
many carriages in the road. He entered the
churchyard and walked to the door of the
church, and stood there in silent waiting.
Suddenly above him the bells clashed out
again with a very cascade of cheerful noise,
and the church poured forth its people. He
had eyes only for the wedded pair; and now
they came, the bride and bridegroom, Maud
leaning on her husband's arm. He could
have put his hand upon her as she passed
him. His brother Will looked him in the
face with his own eyes full of joyful pride and
kindness to the world, and had no more thought
of him or knowledge of him at that second
than if he had never existed. An old woman,
scarlet cloaked, who stood beside Frank, cried
out, 'God bless *you*, Madam Fairholt!' in
a quavering old voice with tears in it; and
Maud's placid eyes passed Frank's face as
they thanked the well-wisher. For a mere
second of time the soft eyes rested upon him;
but it was enough. Calm, good, gentle, almost
angelic, they seemed. Grief had made a home

there long, and had left signs of his dwelling
behind him. Her delicate beauty had none
of its old atmosphere of vivacity. There
were one or two straight lines upon her forehead, and her face was paler than it had used
to be. Yet she seemed wonderfully little
changed; and he could see that the ancient
sorrow had departed. The bells clashed on,
the people cheered; the little procession had
passed him. Her image dwelt with him. He
could set them side by side, his lover who
was almost a child, his brother's wife who
was so sweetly grave a woman. In their
society he turned his back upon the pealing
bells and set out for London.

He wept often by the way, for he was
weak, and the fountain of his tears was full.
But whereas of old they had rested within him
like a veritable pool of hell, and had tortured
him with their scaldings, they fell now like
the dew upon Hermon. And this heart-
broken saint, who had sinned so terribly,
and so sorely suffered, went back to the sad
congregation to whom he ministered, and
dwelt among them, waiting with yearning
patience until it should please God to lead
him to the grave.

CHAPTER X.

AUTOBIOGRAPHY.

' Do you know that man ?'

AT this time my sole friend, except for Gascoigne, and almost my sole acquaintance, was Æsop. Gascoigne was always dearer; but circumstances held us apart, and he was not a friend for common loves and uses. In my trouble at his disappearance, I naturally sought out Gregory; and to him I told the story of the Tabernacle, and of Gascoigne's appearance there, and his sudden illness. He was silent and attentive; and when I had finished, he said with great gravity, 'Do all you can to find him.'

'I hope,' I answered, 'that there will be no great difficulty about finding him. My only fear is that his excitement, or his fall, or both together, may have unbalanced his intellect, and that he has gone wandering off unconsciously, or under some delusion.'

'Wait,' said Gregory. 'Let us make pictures.'

'Let us do what?' I asked.

He smiled gravely. 'When I want to understand a thing that puzzles me, I form all manner of mental tableaux. I make the actors in any human problem pose for me whilst I examine them. I daresay I am oftener wrong than right; but I find the practice a good one sometimes. It was wet last night?'

'It rained heavily,' I answered.

'Did it rain when you led Gascoigne to the cab?'

'Fast,' I told him.

'Did you wrap him up well, before leading him to the cab?'

'Not at all,' I answered. 'He was bareheaded, for one thing.'

'Did anybody put his hat into the cab after you? No? That was what I wanted to suggest to you. He would buy a hat, or go through the streets bareheaded, or take one of yours. Let us go to the Inn, and see which of the three he did.'

The porter of the Inn had seen a gentleman without a hat pass out at the gates, and had seen him cross to the hatter's shop at the opposite corner. There was a clue, said Æsop. But the clue led us no farther than the hatter's shop. The shopman had sold a black wide-awake hat to a young clergyman, who had come in bareheaded from Clement's Inn, and had afterwards walked down Fleet Street.

'That tells us little,' I said in a disappointed tone.

'It tells us this,' said Gregory, 'that he was at least collected enough to be mindful of appearances. Now, either a sane man or a mad man might think of replacing a lost hat; but a man whose intellect was disturbed by the shock of a fall would never dream of it. He has gone away with his eyes open, for his own reasons.'

'I remember that you said of Latazzi that a man who theorised had no right to call himself a detective.'

'I am not theorising—much,' said Gregory. 'I have better grounds to go on than that fool of a detective had.' He had quite a savage despite for Mr. Latazzi, and for the whole detective force private and public.'

'What are your grounds?' I asked anxiously. 'Tell me.'

'No,' he said; 'I will not tell you—yet. It will be bad enough when it comes!'

'What do you mean?' I cried. 'You are not used to talk without a meaning; but I can see none.'

'I had no right to say what I have said already,' Gregory replied, 'and I can say no more. *Nous verrons*, my friend—*nous verrons*. You sha'n't fret about that fellow, with his cranks and twists and changeful tempers. Leave him alone. He has come to no harm.'

'But he was really ill last night,' I pleaded, grieved at Gregory's contemptuous tone, and angered by it also, as I had a right to be in my friend's defence.

'He was well enough this morning, I have no doubt,' said Gregory with a harshness of manner which surprised me. 'And the beggar walked off without saying good-bye—that was all. He had his reasons for it, I daresay, and you'll know them some day.'

'What is the reason of this sudden tone about Gascoigne?' I demanded, grieved and hurt.

'Is it sudden?' asked Æsop, turning one

quick glance upon me. This set me thinking
that the change between the friends was one
of long standing, and that I had blinded myself
to it.

'How long is it,' I said, 'since you quarrelled ?'

'We have not quarrelled,' Gregory replied.
'But I have been guilty of a good deal of
hypocrisy about the matter, and I must end it
now. I will not tell you whose fault it is, or
how it came about ; but Gascoigne and I have
not been friends for many a year, and will be
friends no more, as long as this life lasts.'

I suppose that my tenderness for Gascoigne
would have made this revelation hard to bear
at any time ; but now when I had seen him
in pain and illness, and whilst I was so uncertain about him, it angered me, even coming
from Gregory.

'I expected this,' I said, 'or some of it.
What did you do to Gascoigne ?'

'I did that to Gascoigne,' he answered
slowly, 'for which, if he has a soul at all, he
should be grateful all his life.—Jack '—he put
both hands upon my shoulders — 'trust me.
Wait. Be in no hurry to hurt yourself.'

'Gregory,' I answered, deeply wounded

' these innuendoes are unworthy of you. However Gascoigne and you have quarrelled—'

'We have never quarrelled,' he answered ; but I went on :

' Let me keep *my* esteem for you, at least.'

'Gascoigne is an older friend of yours than I am,' he answered with a smile, in which I seemed dimly to read many things—sadness and a very kind regard amongst them ; ' but we have liked each other, you and I, and we have been pretty thick together. Have I spoken one hard word about your friend ?'

'Why should you speak hard words about him ?' I demanded.

' I have not spoken them,' he said quietly. ' But you think me hard because I tell you not to grieve about him until you are compelled to grieve.'

' Shall I be compelled to grieve ?' I felt the words, as I spoke them, like a challenge.

He answered me sadly, almost solemnly, ' I am afraid you will.'

My mind grasped an awful fancy. ' Is Gascoigne,' I cried, and paused—' is Gascoigne— mad ?' His eloquence had not been that of sober reason. His appearance at the Tabernacle was singular, and not easy to account for. I seemed suddenly to remember an emphasis in Gregory's words as we left the hatter's shop a little while before—'Either a sane man or a mad man.' I gave myself no time to think that this would not account for Gregory's insinuations, but spoke out the fear when I saw it.

'No, Jack, no!' he said gravely.

'Then why,' I cried, 'do you play upon me with these doubts and suspicions, these hints of trouble and mischief, which might go to make up a Tragedy of Errors? Look you, Gregory. You have been a friend of mine for years, a good friend and a true friend until now. But I have loved Gascoigne ever since I can remember, and have loved him almost better than anybody in the world. If you have any suspicion of him, let me know it, and I will work harder to clear him than I have worked to clear myself. Could anything look darker than the case against me? Even if it were anything as vile as that, let me know—though indeed, Gregory, the viler the suspicion is, the better I shall like it, for the surer I shall be it is not true.'

'Jack,' he said, 'let us leave the theme. I am sorry that it has cropped up between us.'

'It may not be a great thing now,' I answered, accepting his simile; 'but if we walk
along on our respective sides, we shall find
it large enough to shut us out of sight of
each other.'

'Very well,' Gregory replied. 'We shall
meet at the far end of it; and you will be
sorry for the side you took.'

'I take my side at once,' I said miserably;
'I will hold no doubt of Gascoigne.'

He brought down his hand heavily upon
the table, for we were seated in my chambers
during the greater part of this conversation.
Looking up at him, I saw an expression of
resolve upon his face, which frightened me,
in spite of my trust in Gascoigne. 'Have
you been in the habit of keeping Gascoigne's
letters?' he asked.

'I have a few of them,' I answered, trembling without knowing why.

'Bring one or two with you, and come with
me. Obliterate date and signature, if you
desire to shield him.'

'Is that your accusation?' I cried in a
stormy rage and triumph. 'Put it to the
test! And when you have proved it false—
and prove it false you shall—we will go our

ways without hand-shakings.   This is the end
of all your innuendoes.   Come; I am ready.'
I had caught up a bundle of letters whilst
speaking, and had drawn out two or three in
Gascoigne's handwriting.

Gregory stood before me with his lips set
tight, and his eyes gleaming, not with anger,
but with tears.   'Jack,' he said gently, 'I have
never been so sorry for anybody in all my
life.   It had to come.   It was only just that
it should come, and I knew before Sunday
night that it was coming.'

His manner disconcerted me, and threw a
chill of doubt upon me.   No; I never doubted
Gascoigne.   'Before Sunday night?' I said,
speaking as scornfully as I could, to hide my
fears.   'More mysteries?   Or are you mad?
What had Sunday night to do with it?'

'I heard Gascoigne on Sunday night, my
poor lad,' he aswered.   I hated Æsop for
the pity in his voice, which seemed so certain
of the misery before me.   'You noticed the
burst of self-accusation in his sermon there?
That clinched the nail a little harder; but it
was driven pretty tightly in beforehand.'

'Why, you suspicious madman,' I exclaimed,
'have you no conception of the saintliness of

soul which makes one little blot of evil-living look as though it soiled a life ? '

' I know,' he answered steadily and kindly, ' that there is such a thing. But there is a religion—the best some men can reach to— which is all remorse and ecstasy ; which has no foundation except in the emotions ; which can soar with the saint, and fall with the fool. I know a man whose remorse for a great fault, committed in his boyhood, nearly drove him mad, whose horror of himself and of his crime was as terrible as it was real ; a man whose hopes were high, whose capacities were large, a man of ripe scholarship and amazing elo- quence, who did again in manhood the thing which made him loathe himself in youth ; and having done it, cast his hopes to the winds, and threw himself a waif upon the world. And he set himself,' said Gregory, laying a finger on my breast as he faced me, ' this task —to preach to the vulgar, whom his dainty instincts made hateful to him—to live among them in ministration to their needs—to point them to heights of hope which he believed were lost to him for ever. And it happened at the beginning of his speech one night that he saw the man before him whom he had

wronged in youth. The sight almost broke
him down; but he struggled with himself—
hear me out—and beat his fears down, and
went on, until in the full flow of his speech
he caught the eyes of the friend he had
wronged by the same crime in manhood, and
fell back, crushed and broken.—Do you know
that man ? '

Gregory's voice had grown to an earnestness which bore me down. I was compelled
to listen, though I pretended to pay little
heed at first. I strove to close my mind's
eyes to that picture of the school cricket-
field which forced itself upon them, and I
struggled not to read the picture's meaning.
' Who is your man ? ' I asked; but though I
tried to throw the scorn I would fain have
felt into my voice, my own sick terror sounded
there instead.

' The man is your dearest friend,' said
Gregory.

' I'll not believe it ! ' I cried passionately.
' I will give no credence to it for a second.
He's the soul of truth and honour, and it is
not possible that he should have done such
a thing.' I saw less plainly the room in which
we stood than I saw the school cricket-ground

with its two figures in the moonlight. I heard
even whilst I was speaking the stern pity of
my old schoolmaster's voice. Gascoigne had
cast himself face downwards on the grass, and
I was creeping guiltily away again, when
Gregory's voice recalled me.

'It is very terrible that your clearance from
the charge against you should come in this
way. I know how hard it is ; and I have
held suspicion back from you, and would
almost have held back certainty if you would
have let me.'

'I shall not clear my friend by raging
against the accusation,' I said in answer, trying hard to keep my voice unshaken, and to
believe that I believed the story false. 'You
shall tell me all your grounds for this miserable
suspicion, and I will make it my business to
remove them one by one.'

'You shall hear them all,' he answered, still
standing sadly before me, and speaking in a
reluctant sulky voice, which I can understand
better now than I could at the time. 'A
month before Gascoigne left school, a cheque
in my father's name, bearing my indorsement,
was presented at the bank. The people there
saw some reason to doubt my father's signa-

ture, and consulted with him. He denied the cheque, and came to see me about it. Less hasty than your uncle, he had faith in me; and the matter was investigated, with this result—that Gascoigne was brought to confession a day before his time at school expired; that we three—the doctor, my father, and I—agreed to hold our tongues, hoping and believing that his remorse and shame would teach him a lesson not to be forgotten; and that he went away scot-free. When this last business came, I knew that Gascoigne had been living at a rate unwarranted by his income; and I had been fearing a smash of some sort, though nothing so terrible as this. When it was decided that the indorsement of the cheque was really in your hand-writing, and I knew that the cheque was written on blank paper, my suspicions jumped in the old direction. When I heard, as I did two months ago, that Gascoigne had disappeared from his curacy, suspicion grew stronger. When I heard again that a young preacher on the Surrey side, who did not allow his name to be announced, was drawing vast congregations, and was talking in a certain vein of inspired half-madness which I thought I knew, I went to hear and see him. I found, as I expected I should find, that this was Gascoigne. I meant to speak to him that night, and tax him with my new suspicions; but I saw you struggling through the crowd towards the platform, and I held back. I went again last night, and planted myself a little to one side in the front row, and he saw me when he came in; and the sight of me nearly broke him down. But he fought through, and was forgetting me—or had forgotten me, when I saw suddenly in his face the look—the very look—which met us when my father and I waited for him in the doctor's study, and when he knew at a glance the purpose which brought us there. And I guessed then, when I heard your cry and saw you rushing towards him, what I know now—that he had seen you as well as me, and that the accusation of your presence crushed him like a sudden weight.'

What could I say or do? Of what avail was it to believe that he had not wronged me, since he had wronged another? He had called Gregory his friend.

'I am bitterly grieved for your sake,' Æsop said; but I turned away in the misery of my heart, and vowed inwardly that I would trust no man any more, or woman either. ' But you at least shall be cleared.'

' Cleared ? ' I answered bitterly. ' What does it matter whether I am cleared or not ? I would rather never have been cleared than have known — this — Why talk about it ? Let the whole business slide. Let us hear no more of it. One or two of us are honest, maybe. Let us leave the rogues alone. Oh, Æsop, Æsop, this will break my heart !'

He made no answer, but sat down and began to smoke. I followed his example after a while, boasting to myself that I was beginning to know the world and value it aright. We kept silence for perhaps an hour.

' You must be cleared, Jack,' said Æsop at last. ' I don't suppose that Mr. Hartley will want to make a scandal by prosecuting, and I must go down and see him, and tell him what I know.'

' Leave the whole base thing alone,' I responded. ' I can hold no intercourse with Mr. Hartley, and I can accept nothing at his hands. I have no wish to be cleared from his suspicion. Let him find it out for himself, or never find it out at all. It matters nothing to me either way.'

'He loved you for many a year, before he fell into this trap,' said Gregory. 'He has a good kind heart, and his suspicion has been as deep a grief to him as it has been to you. There is nothing which would rejoice him more than the certainty of your innocence. He has a right to know that you are innocent. He has a right to know who is the man who misused his name. Jack, you must be guided by me in this. Indeed, you must.'

So vile—so vile a crime! There on the table lay that letter of indignant sympathy and protest with which he had answered me. So shameful a pretence! So pitiless an hypocrisy! Was it Gascoigne who had done these things? It was horrible—incredible! And I knew that it was true.

'Do as you will,' I answered. 'Nothing matters to me any more in the whole world. Nothing but this one thing—that you exact my uncle's solemn promise that he does not drag Gascoigne'—what an effort it cost me to speak his name—'to open disgrace. And this other thing—that he does not offer me any apology or amends.'

'You cannot forgive an old man who loves you for having broken his own heart over a mistake about you? That is not like you, Jack, and it will not last.'

'It will last my time,' I answered. My soul was full of bitterness.

'I know you better than you know yourself,' quoth Æsop. 'I shall see your uncle and shall try to secure the pledge you ask for.' The postman's knock sounded at the door at that moment, and Gregory rose and brought from the box one letter. 'This is from home,' he said, as he laid it before me. 'I hope it brings good news.' With that he shook hands and left me.

I sat brooding in anger and bitterness long after he had gone, and at length took up the letter from the table. In spite of my misery, the sight of the handwriting made my heart beat; for the letter came from Polly. It ran thus :—

'MY POOR DEAR JACK,—I have just seen Maud, and she has told me everything. I wondered at your silence, and had grown angry at it; but I know everything you have done, and I praise you and admire you for it. You could not have taken his money whilst he retained a suspicion so pro-

digious. Trials are good for all good people.
You would not have done what you are doing
now except for this terrible suspicion. And
now you are going to be famous, and will be
a great author, and delight and instruct us
all. My father has forbidden me to write to
you, for your uncle has told him his abominable story. Or—I ought not to say that,
for I do not really know ; but he has told
him he will not leave you any money.
But I have told him I should disobey him
once, and should write to say I did not
believe you had done anything to deserve
such cruel conduct. Perhaps, after all, papa
does not know anything of that monstrous
and shameful tale ; for I remember he looked
surprised when I spoke of your being cleared.
But take this for comfort — that Maud
believes in you—that I believe in you—that
Will believes in you ; for I asked him, and he
said he did with all his heart. You have not
suffered without sympathy; and whatever
has made Mr. Hartley believe such horrid
nonsense as that you are a forger, you
can afford to be sorry for him, for it has
broken his heart. Maud says he thinks well
of your refusal to take his money, and has

learned from Mr. Gregory which are your
articles, and reads them over and over again,
though he never speaks about them, and will
not allow you to be mentioned. Be courage-
ous, my poor Jack, and go on working, and
believe in the love and constancy of all of us.—
Your affectionate Cousin,   MARY.

'*P.S.*—Maud is to be married on Wednesday.'

Why had Uncle Ben thought it needful to
tell Mr. Fairholt that he would not leave me
any money? The answer was ready — He
had guessed the feelings with which I regarded
Polly. Why should Mr. Fairholt have carried
on the news to her? Again the answer was
clear—He also had guessed the feelings with
which I regarded Polly. I am willing to confess now that a man need scarcely have been
a conjurer to make the guess. The matter
must have been very plain to everybody;
though I had believed with the fatuity common
to young people in love, that the knowledge
of my state of mind was limited to my dozen
of confidants. And now for the first time in
my life I rose up in resolve, and vowed that
I would do my worthiest to win her. At least

I would try to justify some of her belief in me, however her undeserved praises might humble me. I turned to the letter once more, and read the words—' You can afford to be sorry for him, for it has broken his heart,' but in spite of the gentler feelings which Polly's letter had evoked, I refused Uncle Ben my forgiveness, and hardened myself against him.

CHAPTER XI.

' Troman,' said my aunt, ' what have you *to cry for ?'*

I WORKED, and found in work such relief as it could give me. I laboured as I had never done before, and accumulated large stores of journalistic capital. But life had grown to be a bitter business, and I had little heart or hope for anything, or faith in anything. Perhaps there are not many men so happy as to preserve their faith until they reach the age of five-and-twenty. Perhaps those who keep faith longest feel it hardest to lose it. My life had gone smoothly. I had had my dreams—dreaming with my eyes open. Most men had seemed lovable, many admirable, two or three kingly, and one supreme. And when Gascoigne tumbled from his place, my scheme of things went to chaos.

Stunned by that misfortune, I looked stupidly back, and thought even the suspicion which had fallen upon myself easy to bear by comparison. There is no pain like the pain of finding a friend unworthy and untrue. And now for a time I doubted everybody, and nursed a wrath and hatred against the world, by far more foolish than my faith had been.

I prospered in my profession, and men began to speak favourably of me. There are some people, who live altogether out of literary circles, to whom any sort of connection with letters appears to be of extravagant value. Some of my old acquaintances were men of this kind, and showed a disposition to return to me, now that I began to be known. I am afraid that in my new-born cynicism I treated some of them rather uncivilly, though, indeed, they had not deserved well at my hands. I hope I have grown wiser than to quarrel with butterflies for liking sunshine and avoiding shade, though even now the butterfly is scarcely my type of friendship. But it has been said, times out of number, that your convert or pervert is the most sweeping and ' thoroughgoing of men, and I being perverted to cynicism and a wholesale disbelief in good, did my best to embitter myself against every-body in those days, and, in a most unhappy degree, succeeded.

Through all this I clung to Æsop; and he stuck to me with a fidelity not to be shaken or strengthened by any fall or rise of fortune. Seeing how low my general mood had fallen, and how prone I had become to nurse my grudges against the world in private, he pro-posed—on grounds of professed economy—to chum with me and share my chambers; and this being carried into effect, we worked together, breakfasted and dined together, and kept each other in almost constant company. It pleases me now to believe that Gregory worked the better for companionship. He was writing a comedy at this time. I can recall his staid and serious face as he sat apart at a table overspread with scattered manuscripts. I can see him again, rising from his chair to prowl about the room, pipe in mouth, emitting vast clouds of smoke, and rumpling his hair at intervals with both hands, looking as distracted as a condemned criminal. Now and again he would break into wild shouts of laughter, and would execute fantastic dances,

and then, with a countenance of gloom, would
commit his inspirations to paper, and prowl
about once more distractedly. In our literary
work we were both afflicted with a desire for
bodily motion, and we used to cross and re-
cross each other in our thoughtful rambles
over the carpet, until it bore the plain impress
of our feet, and two threadbare and faded
lines ran from end to end of the room. I
believe that Gregory still works in that
manner ; but I confess to having worn it
out, and abandoned it. The work was happier in those days of emotion, when at a
sweet fancy my eyes have seen the lines that
traced it, dimly, or with some half-expressed
sarcasm seething within me, I have had to
leave my table and hammer out the lines with
mutterings and stridings to - and - fro. After
every one of Gregory's laughters, and its
consequent wild war - dance, I was dragged
earthwards from my own clouds whilst he
read over to me scraps of dialogue. ' I think
this 'll fetch 'em, Jack,' was his exordium, and
he would spout the products of his muse's
labours with infinite gusto. An hour later,
he would rise in deep despondency, and an-
nounce his opinion that the whole comedy

was bosh ; and then sitting down despairingly to read it, he would go off into a succession of crackling laughters, which bespoke the intensest relish of his own performance.

It chanced one day that we were both marching up and down the room, hammering in great heat at our respective mental irons, when a timid and uncertain knock sounded at the door ; and Gregory, being nearer than I, answered the summons. Standing in the middle of the carpet, a little disturbed by the interruption, I heard a voice that warmed my heart, and hurrying to the door, found Bob and Sally in the act of entering. The good creature, Sally, embraced me there and then, and shed tears over me, in quite the old familiar manner ; and Mr. Turner shook my hands meanwhile, murmuring, ' Excuse the liberty.' When the first heat of welcome was ended, Gregory closed the outer door ; but Bob, repeating ' Excuse the liberty,' reopened it, and revealed the presence of a small boy, who had hitherto escaped attention. This small boy, who was dressed in black broadcloth of a cumbrous cut, and reminded me quaintly of myself as I had first appeared at Island Hall, was comically like Sally, and had a ridiculous resemblance to Bob, so that I had no difficulty in identifying his relationship.

'This is your boy, Sally?' I inquired.

'Yes, my darlin',' returned Sally, beaming. 'He's the eldest. Come in, Johnny.'

I had not seen him for some four or five years; and he had so far outgrown his remembrances of me, that on my offering to shake hands with him, he retired in much apparent discomfiture behind his father's legs.

'Johnny's his naam,' said Bob in the old broad dialect, which always sounds in my ears like a memory of childhood. 'Excuse the liberty, young mister, but the missis, her would naam him after yo.' Bob himself was dressed in black broadcloth, and I believe had had his hair curled for his visit to the metropolis. I cannot actually pledge myself to the accuracy of that surmise; but I know that he had a long and half-unfolded roll of curl upon the very top of his head, which I could not remember to have seen there before. This ornament displayed a treacherous inclination to stand bolt upright; and Bob becoming conscious of that fact, smoothed it furtively with his broad palm; but it arose

again and again, and gave him, in conjunc-
tion with his dark clothes and his solemnity
of visage, something of the aspect of a cocka-
too in mourning. Gregory and I cleared a
table, and laid out a refection of wine and
biscuits ; and Sally, who wore a bonnet like
a flower-show, and a shawl like a rainbow,
sat in her gloves in great grandeur, and
sipped and nibbled in the most ladylike and
superior manner. Bob—what with the clothes
and the curl, and the strange rooms, and
Gregory's presence—was in a sort of patient
agony of uneasiness. Gregory was quick to
discern the discomfiture he inflicted upon my
visitors, and feigning business in a little while
went out. Shortly afterwards, Bob arose, and
obscuring the obdurate curl with a hat so
stiff and shiny it might have been of steel
japanned, also withdrew, announcing his intention of taking a look at Temple Bar. He
led away my young namesake by the hand,
promising to return in half-an-hour, and I
was left alone with Sally.

'An' now, my precious,' said Sally, all her
company manners vanishing, and her good
self returning suddenly. She settled herself
in her chair, and hugged her many-tinted

knees with her gloved hands—'an' now, my precious !'

I cannot easily tell how much good the sight of Sally did me, or how immediate and direct the influence seemed. But she had been so closely knit with all my early life, and from the first to the last of my re-membrances had been so true ; she was so little changed, and brought so vividly back to me the memory of so many gracious acts and happy times, that I should have been hard indeed not to have been somewhat moved by recollection in her presence.

'And now, Sally !' I answered.

'Bob an' me,' said Sally, 'has never had what you might call a reg'lar out sence we was married. An' Bob havin' that pros-pered as to be a master - builder, Master Johnny, a-keepin' on a dozen hands an' doin' well, we made up wer minds as we'd come to London ; an' here we be.'

'And here you are, Sally,' I responded.

'Yes,' said Sally, still hugging her knees, ''an' here we be. An' who do you think we come up in the same train with ?'—I pro-fessed my inability to divine.—'Make a guess,' said Sally, with such a meaning look, that I guessed at once, and asked, 'Not Cousin Polly?'

'Yes,' said my old nurse, nodding like a toy - mandarin—'your Cousin Polly, Master Johnny. She come up in the same train along o' we, with your aunt; an' she was a-lookin' that beautiful— Well, there!' She lengthened the adjective into 'bee-oo-tiful,' and unclasped her knees and cast her hands abroad when she said, 'Well, there!' as if proclaiming the inability of further words to express the sight.

This news disturbed me; for in spite of all the vows I had made, I could not fail to recognise the gulf which had opened up between Polly and myself. While the expectations my Uncle Ben had taught me to entertain were still with me, there had been no social breech between us; but it seemed as though it would have been a cowardly and cruel thing to ask her to share the broken hopes of fortune and the struggling life which lay before me. Here and there, the prizes of the literary life are large; but I had modesty and sense enough to know that the great prizes were not for men of my calibre; and although I could already see my way, I knew

well enough that there was no golden goal at
the end of it. The life before me was a life
of labour and of narrowed means. Single, I
could get on well enough; but I could not endure the thought of narrowed means for Polly,
and love's sweet dream was coming near the
end and growing bitter. In the pleasure of
welcoming my old friend, I had forgotten my
troubles; but this mention of Polly's name
brought them all back in full tide.

'Why, Johnny, darlin',' what's the matter?'
cried Sally. 'You're a-lookin' quite downcast,
I declare. What is it?' She came and knelt
before me and took my hands in hers. 'What
is it, Johnny? Theer's nothin' amiss between
you an' your cousin, is theer?'

'Sally,' I answered, 'this is not a thing to
be talked of; but I can trust you, I know.
I am a poor man now, and work for my
living, like many other people. All my life
is changed, and a good many of my old
hopes are thrown away — and that among
them.'

'No,' said Sally; 'not if it was to come
to a crust o' dry bread an' a glass o' water.'

I did not understand her, or pay any great
heed to her words; but I repeated that my

life was changed, and that many of my old hopes were thrown away.

'*Not* that among 'em, Johnny,' said Sally. 'Not if you was to be as poor as Job. You couldn't have the heart!'. I did not understand at all, and I suppose my face expressed it. 'Johnny,' she said with an air of serious admonition, 'when a young gentleman's been keepin' company with a young lady all his life, he ought to ask her if she's willin' to part, afore he goes away, whatever happens.'

'My dear Sally,' I answered, 'you do not understand. I have never spoken a word to my cousin which would make her think—'

'Words, my foolish precious!' returned Sally, shaking her head as she knelt, still holding my hands, before me. 'Why, what's words? Actions speaks louder than words, my darlin.' Do you fancy as she don't know? An' you remember, Johnny,' she went on with a general plea for the whole sex, 'as we poor women's tongues is tied. It's you to speak first.'

'No,' I responded; 'it is not for me to speak at all. Had things gone differently, I should have spoken ; but not now—not now.'

'How old are you, Johnny?' asked Sally suddenly.

'Five-and-twenty,' I responded. 'Nearly a quarter of a century, Sally. That sounds quite old.'

'Miss Mary's more than two years younger,' said Sally. 'Over two-an'-twenty. Most ladies is married younger than that, my dear, ain't 'em? What's she a-waiting for? How many offers has she throwed away? O Johnny, my silly darlin,' to be so blind!'

Could it be true? Sally spoke with the confidence of conviction, and my own heart was eager to believe. And yet, and yet I scarcely dared to think it. And yet, and yet there was no escape from hope.

'Sally,' I said in much agitation, 'you speak as if you were certain.'

'So I am,' she answered, kneeling before me still. 'You must tell her, Johnny, and ask her to wait for you.'

I arose from my seat and paced the room excitedly. 'Yes,' I said at length; 'I will speak. I will ask, and know the truth.'

At that instant there came another summons at the door; and thinking that this was Bob come back again, I left Sally to open it, and not caring to be seen just then, retired to my bedroom.

'*You* here, Troman?' said my Aunt Bertha's voice. 'How do you do?' My aunt's voice came nearer. 'Where is Mr. Campbell?'

'I am here,' I cried, 'and will come to you in a moment.' I drank a glass of water, and composed myself; then re-entering the sitting-room, met Cousin Polly's candid eyes and outstretched hand. This apparition coming upon me in so unprepared and emotional a condition, found me quite helpless. 'We speak,' I said, 'of angels, and they show their wings.'

'Troman,' said my aunt when our greetings were over, 'you are the very woman I want to speak to. I have something serious to say to you.—John, take your cousin for a stroll through the Temple Gardens while I talk to Troman. Don't hurry back. I've a great deal to say to her.'

I submitted tamely to be driven from my own chambers by this overwhelming aunt; and Polly came with me. We crossed the roaring Strand, and walked into the quiet of the gardens. There were few people there. A few nurse-girls, a scattered handful or so of children, a Blue Coat Boy walking along bareheaded, and reading as he went. As we passed him, I looked down, and saw that the book was the Essays of Elia ; surely the fittest book in the world to read in the Temple Gardens. I am always too shamefaced to do those things, but I should have liked to have tipped that Blue Coat Boy on the spot. Polly saw the book as well as I.

'Elia was a good creature,' she said. 'If I lived in London, I should come here a great deal ; and I fancy that he would be oftener in one's thoughts than any one else associated with the place. Are you often here ?'

'Often,' I answered. 'But not to think of Elia.'

'You are an author now,' she said, 'and have many thoughts. I have often wondered —tell me—do you write to the world impersonally ? If I were an author, I think I should never be able to do that. I should write as if I were writing a letter, and I should have some one in my mind who would be sure to understand my mood—Maud, for instance, or Will, or you, or somebody who had known me all my life. It would be easier to write so, I fancy, than to scatter one's bread upon the waters, without knowing who might taste it.'

'I have written all that I *have* written,' I responded, 'for one reader only, and I have looked to my audience of one to keep me at my best, and to shut out everything unworthy from my work.' I felt her eyes upon me, and, glancing at her, saw upon her face a look which was difficult to define. I thought it a little troubled, and feared she read my meaning, and was sorry for it. But I had resolved to speak, and I went on : 'I have had that one reader always in my mind and in my heart, and she has ruled my life.' We were walking slowly side by side, and there was no one near us. The Blue Coat Boy was deep in Elia, fifty yards behind. ' Polly ! I have loved you ever since I can remember you. I have had no hope or ambition which you have not governed. I am poor now, and I have to fight the world ; but you have given me heart and hope to fight it. I have struggled day by day to be a little worthier to love you.'

'Jack !' she said in a pained voice appealingly.

'I was wrong to speak,' I said a moment later. 'Forget that I have spoken.'

'No,' she answered softly ; it is not that.

You make me feel ashamed. I am a wayward, foolish girl, and you speak of being—'

'I love you,' I answered; 'that is all the worthiness I have.' We walked a little further in silence. 'Tell me—it will but cost a word—if I can hope?'

I was looking down at her bent and averted face as we walked. She turned her head, and looked me bravely in the eyes, though brow and cheek and throat were blushing, and her own eyes were moist.

'Hope for my love, Jack?' she asked.

'Yes.'

'Be sure of it.' Her eyes brimmed over, the sweet blush faded as she spoke, and she drooped her head again.

We walked in silence for a long time, and walked so slowly, that the Blue Coat Boy, still poring upon Elia, following the path we took, went past us. I have often smiled to think how narrow an escape that Boy had from great astonishment. I felt an almost irresistible desire to endow him at one stroke with all the money then in my possession. My invariable want of promptitude on small occasions robbed the boy of a splendid tip, and

me of a great relief. But I was grateful to
him, and felt affectionately towards him, for
I remembered that it was his Elia which had
opened the conversation between Polly and
myself. The Blue Coat Boy is quite a young
man by this time. He has probably given
up the pursuit of literature in the Temple
Gardens, and walks, perchance, in Groves of
Academe by classic Cam or Isis. But if
this should meet his eye, I beg him to accept
a gratitude which has lost none of its flavour
by a little keeping. If he will favour us with
a visit, my wife and I will make him welcome. He has never guessed it, but all this
time he has been one of our Lares.

It was quite dark when we turned to go
back to Clement's Inn ; and when we reached
my chambers, Aunt Bertha and Sally were
sitting in the gloom alone.

'Has your husband lost himself, Sally ? ' I
inquired.

'He's took Johnny to the circus,' responded
Sally. 'I didn't want to go away 'ithout
seein' you again.'

'You have been away a pretty time, young
people,' said Aunt Bertha with severity. But

by this time and in this society I was prepared to encounter reproof with a forehead as of brass.

'Aunt Bertha,' I answered, drawing Polly's arm through mine, 'you may be assumed to stand *in loco parentis* towards Polly. And Sally, who is the best and most faithful creature in the world, as everybody knows, may be assumed to stand in the same relationship towards myself. And in your presence, I confess that the two indiscreet young people whom you may now dimly behold—'

'Don't be prolix,' said Aunt Bertha. Sally had risen, and was standing near the window with her hands clasped. Now that I come to think of it, I do not believe that Sally understood one word I said, except perhaps her own praises ; but she understood the situation, and showed the fact by a gasp of genuine emotion. At that signal, Polly withdrew her hand—Aunt Bertha rose to meet her—and in less time than it takes to tell it, they were crying for joy in one another's arms. Sally of course was weeping over me ; and for my own manhood's sake, I was thankful for the gloom.

'Troman,' said my aunt, what have *you* to

cry for ? '—Sally returned no answer.—' Do you
think that Mr. Campbell is throwing himself
away ? '

'Oh ma'am,' cried Sally, 'haven't I knowed
and loved 'em both sence they was babies ? '

'Troman,' said my aunt, advancing to her,
'you are a good creature, and you have a
beautiful heart.' And with that commenda-
tion, Aunt Bertha positively kissed Sally, and
made her, as I believe, the proudest woman
in the United Kingdom. When we had all
toned down again, I was about to light the
lamp ; but my aunt forbade me ; and in a little
time Sally took her leave, promising to call
again on the morrow.

'Did Troman tell you anything, John ? '
asked my aunt, before Sally's footsteps had
left the stairs.

'Yes,' I answered, sheltered by the friendly
darkness, sitting with Polly's hand in mine ;
'she told me to do what I have done.'

'Should you have done it, if she had not
told you to do it ? ' asked my aunt.

'No,' I answered ; 'I should not have
dared.'

'Then for once,' said my aunt triumphantly,
'a match-making old woman was right.   I

ordered Troman to come and tell you. And now '—she hurried on, as if to prevent either of us from speaking—' I want to say a word about your future. My brother Robert will object. — Mary, be quiet. Your father will object. Well, if you must know, he objects already. But I have saved a good deal of money, and I have my own fortune, and I have made my will, and left it all to John on condition that you marry. — Don't speak a word, but find my bonnet. I don't know whether you will ever think of dining any more, but I am starving. Let us go home and ask Mrs. Brand for some dinner. We are staying with Dr. Brand, and you can come, too, if you like, John.'

Two or three hours later we were seated in Dr. Brand's parlour. The doctor was called away, and Mrs. Brand followed him from the room.

Polly, rising, drew aside the blind. 'What lovely moonlight!' she said, after looking out for a minute or two. 'I don't think I ever saw moonlight look so beautiful before.'

' My dear,' said Aunt Bertha, rising and kissing her, ' the moonlight has grown brighter for happy lovers, ever since the world began.'

CHAPTER XII.

AUTOBIOGRAPHY.

It was no fortuitous likeness, but a portrait.

LET me write down my words again. In all the devious ways in which my life has been guided, I can but recognise a Master Hand. I have been moved inexorably, here and there, against my will, apart from my will. The plan of my life has no more been mine than the words written by my pen this moment are dictated by it. And now in the halting-place of life at which I tell this story, I can see the plan which my unwilling movements here and there have traced, and I know that I was guided to a settled end.

It was a good and wholesome thing that I had to work for a living, and that my work was of such a character that it could not be done without a certain abstraction from all

other thoughts than those which concerned it.
It happened thus that the poison brought its
own antidote. I was daily in some haunt of
poverty or vice ; and I set myself to show
that part of the world for which I worked how
the world outside it lived and felt and thought.
How are the rich and prosperous to know
how to be merciful to the poor, if the press
give the poor no voice ? It is not three
months since I learned for the first time in my
life that there are thousands of people in
England to whom railways are a real and a
terrible grievance. There are countless problems in the life of the very poor of which
the world has no conception, can have no
conception. I set myself to learn the more
urgent of those problems, and to lay them out
for popular study, believing that in the multi-
tude of counsellors there is wisdom, and that
the solutions were likelier to be got at in that
way than in any other.

I found one of the most troublesome of
these problems on its way to a solution in the
hands of an old acquaintance—Mr. Hastings,—
who had purchased one of the worst human
rookeries in all London, and had transformed
it into decency. The place is known as Bolter's

Rents, and stands on the south side of Oxford Street. There is a way through from it to the Seven Dials; and there are intermediate homes of villainy in the midst of which it is even now unsafe for a well-dressed stranger to show himself alone in broad daylight. It was one of the natural results of my occupation that I was 'known to the police;' and a sergeant of the force told me the history of Bolter's Rents so far as he knew it.

'I was on duty close by there,' said the sergeant, 'years ago, when it was a real dangerous place to go into in the daytime. You mayn't believe it, but I was with the present proprietor when he made his first entry into the place. I was on duty in the night-time when he come up to me with a doctor. Theer was a feller took hill in the Rents; and the gentleman—Mr. Hastings were his name, and I daresay you've heard of him—had been down with a nigger-servant which he kep' at that time, which is since dead, I b'leeve. The doctor akshally wouldn't go down without a hofficer; and I went down with 'em; an' it turned out in the hoddest way that Mr. Hastings knowed the sick party, which had come down in the world, from bein' a money-lender in the City, terrible. He's a-livin' there now. German Jew he is. Sweeps a crossing near the Marble Harch, and goes by the name of Tasker.'

I was startled to hear this, though I made no remark about it to the sergeant, but kept my knowledge of the man's history to myself.

' Hif,' said the officer, who was very intelligent and very civil, ' you reely desire to 'ave a good look at the place, you can't do better than find out a party by the name of Penkridge, which lives theer. Tell 'im Hi sent you, an' you'll find 'im a civil an' respeckful feller.'

I sought and found the party by the name of Penkridge, who acted as a sort of porter to the place. It was his function to keep order, and to collect payments, and to overlook a certain amount of weekly scrubbing, which had now been for some years one of the fixed ordinances of Bolter's Rents. I found him, as the sergeant had foretold, very civil and respectful.

' I'm quite a reformed party,' he told me in a whining way, which left me not so certain of his reformation as I might have been ; ' I'm quite a brand, plucked from the burning.'

I supposed—to keep him talking—that Mr. Hastings had done much good there.

'Yes,' he answered ; and so has Dr. Brand's good lady, sir ; and Dr. Brand hisself, sir. Oh yes, sir ; but the party's hand wot saved me, sir, lived in the place hisself, sir. It's the Duke, sir, as done most o' the good as 'as been done 'ere, sir. It was 'im as made me sign the pledge, sir, an' kep me a tee-tot'ler this last five year. Ah sir, if ever there was a saint as was a Dockman, it's poor Mister Jones.'

'Do you call Mr. Jones "The Duke?"' I asked him.

'Oh, I do assure you, sir,' said Penkridge, 'he's quite the gentleman. They say as he had a million of money, sir, and lost it on the turf. Of course, sir, he's quite a poor person now, sir ; but he needn't have been so, sir, if he'd ha' liked ; for many a time, sir, Mr. Hastings have said to me—"Penk-ridge," he says, "I wish you'd ask the Duke to live here altogether an' attend to the Rents," he says, "an' leave them docks for good," he says.'

'And the Duke won't leave?' I asked. 'How is that?'

'Well, sir, it's like this,' said Penkridge.
'He doesn't like to be beholden to nobody.
Not as he's proud. Oh, I do assure you,
not at all, sir. But he's got that way with
him, sir, and the kindest 'art as ever breathed.'

The man told him in his own whining way
many stories of this broken millionaire's kindness and generosity ; and when I left him,
and passed from one room to another, I found
that a mere mention of 'the Duke' drew forth
praises. My curiosity to see so remarkable
a personage, natural in itself, was stimulated
by the constant statement, in answer to my
inquiries, that he would speak to nobody but
the inmates of the court. Mrs. Brand, her
husband, the landlord, city missionaries, Bible
readers—in all a score of people or more,
had attempted to hold intercourse with him.
He was, except for charity, a hermit, and
was quite unapproachable. I determined that
I would seek an interview with him ; and
consulted Penkridge, who responded, that
Mr. Jones had gone into the country ; saying he might be away a week. This was
the first occasion on which he had spent a
night away from the place, since he first
came to it, many years before.

'But, sir,' said Penkridge, under the sooth-
ing influence of a shilling, 'If you'd like to
see the party's rooms, sir, I've got a key as
ud let you in, sir.' .

My curiosity had been so keenly stimulated
concerning the man, that I resolved at least
to see the place in which he lived. Penkridge
led the way up several flights of stairs to a
dark landing; and inserting his key, admitted
me to a chamber with a sloping roof, a clean-
scoured floor, and whitewashed walls. A low
trestle-bed, with coarse but clean clothing; a
chest like a sailor's; a frying-pan, a teapot,
a cup and saucer; a plate, with knife, fork,
and spoon beside it; one chair and a little
table — were all the room contained. The
wall had been scratched in one place; and
the powdered whitewash lay in a line along
the floor, below it. I walked across, and
without any purpose which I can recall, looked
at the place which had been so cleaned; and
Penkridge volunteered the statement that the
inmate of the room was 'allays a-drorin' on
the walls, an' scratchin' out of what he drored.'

'He used to do it when I lived 'ere with
him, sir,' said Penkridge in his whining way.
Faces he'd dror, an' ladies an' gentlemen;

pretty near allays the same ladies an' gentlemen, sir; and one 'ouse he used to dror, an'
trees. an' things. I've told 'im many's the
time, sir, as he might ha' made five shillin'
a day if he'd ha' took to drorin' on the pavement, sir.'

'An artist?' I said lightly, as we left the
room.

'You may well say that, sir,' my guide answered, locking the door behind him. 'You
may well say that, sir, I do assure you, sir.
I've got a take-off as he did o' me, sir, as
couldn't be drored truer, not if it was photy-
graphed, sir.'

I said I should like to see it; and on my
way out I paused at his door, and waited
for the production of this work of art. He
brought a half-sheet of dirty letter-paper; and
I looked at it listlessly; but my eyes had
no sooner fallen upon the paper than my
listlessness had vanished. It was an absolute
and amazing likeness, and was produced by
the least effort conceivable. The man who
could have done this might have made a
fortune as a caricaturist. It was drawn in
that effective outline of which Wallis Mackay
is the latest master, an outline which gives

shadow and rotundity. I bought it for half
a-crown, and carried it away with me. It
hangs before me now, a memento of that
tragedy which it was my destiny to trace to
its close.

Gregory had, after an enforced and lengthy
waiting, fulfilled his promise; and this visit
to Bolter's Rents was made on the Saturday
on which he visited Hartley Hall. He came
back late that night, and gave me in full
the result of his interview with my uncle.
He told me that Uncle Ben had at first
obstinately refused to listen to any evidence
upon the case, saying that it had cost him
grief enough and more, already.

'He said the endorsement was yours,' said
Gregory, 'and that he knew it for yours, in
spite of all the evidence in the universe. I
told him that I admitted that; but that the
forgery was not; and that you had been
fraudulently tricked into signing your name
upon that sheet of paper. He answered in
great excitement, that if I would prove that,
he would give me a hundred thousand pounds;
and said he would draw out a cheque for it
that minute, and hand it over when I made
the proof clear. I told him in answer to

that,' said Gregory, with a wink, 'that he'd better wait until the case *was* proved; and that 'then, if he liked, I wasn't too proud to be set down for a trifle in his will.'

The gist of Gregory's narrative lay in the fact that Uncle Ben was at that moment in London, whither he had come for the purpose of examining the forged signature, which he admitted he had not yet critically looked into, except so far as to enable him to pronounce it an imitation of his own. He had heard the story of Gascoigne's perfidy; but had promised that, if I wished it, and the tale proved true, he would let him go, and take no steps against him.

All this brought but little consolation to my spirit; and indeed, I would rather have continued to bear the blame, than have had it removed from me, to be transferred in such an unexampled load of treachery and baseness to Gascoigne's shoulders. Crime is a plant which has a thousand-thousand seeds, that fly, loose as thistle-down, and wide as the bounds of human circumstance can carry them, to breed corruption in uncounted hearts. Revenge distrust, and many ulcers more were bred in me from the seeds of Gascoigne's guilt. I had cast away love and worship, and felt as though there were no more to give, and all men were unworthy.

When I remember what happened on the following Monday, I am filled with shame. But I am bound, if I tell this tale at all, to tell it fairly, and I set down that with the rest. I was alone in my chambers, and sore at heart, thinking of Gascoigne's villainy and Uncle Ben's faithlessness, when there came a knock at the outer door, and I found my Uncle Ben standing there. I gave him no greeting; and he followed me into my sitting-room, and set his hat and stick upon the table. I sat down, and would not look at him; and he stood there for a little time in silence. Then he cleared his throat once or twice, and called me by name. I made no answer; and again there was a silence for a space.

'Johnny,' he said at length, relapsing in his emotion—which surely should have touched me—into a broader accent than I had ever heard him use till now—'I've come to ax your pardon. Theer's no moor doubt about the matter. I do't suppose theer ever was anny; but I acted wrong, Johnny. We've hunted that theer Gascoigne up, an' we've found him out; and he's confessed; an' I've come straight up from him t'ax your pardon. I've let him off, for your sake, Johnny; and I've come up t'ax your pardon.'

His voice melted me, but I would not speak. I am ashamed to tell the truth; but it was this, and this only, which held me back from meeting him at once with open arms. I was miserably afraid that men would say—or think, if they did not say it in my hearing—that had Uncle Ben been poor, I could have had no forgiveness for the wrongful suspicion he had held; but that since he was rich, I forgave him freely. And this fear held me silent whilst he waited, and silent still as his appeal went on.

'Johnny,' he said again, 'it broke my heart to think it of you. Be mine the shame, Johnny; it ain't no shame to you. Throw it all on me. I'll bear it. I deserve it. But I will say this, as never a uncle loved his nevew better in this wide world than I did. It broke my heart to think it of you. I take all the shame an' blame o' what I did, an' I take it glad an' willin'— glad an' willin'. I couldn't bear to think it o' my sister's child.'

His voice broke, and he paused again;

and I knew that he was weeping. Pride filled my heart, and though his tears should surely have touched me, I held my peace, and answered not a word.

'You're hard, to be so young,' he said again, after a long pause. 'But I deserve it. Oh, I deserve it; but it ain't what I looked for. I'm gettin' old. I ain't long for this world. You won't turn me away without a word. You won't let me go away without sayin', " Uncle, I forgive you!" I acknowledge as I was a wrong-headed old fool to think my lad 'ud dream o' such a thing. But I've suffered for it, Johnny; I've suffered for it.'

Still my pride kept me silent, and he stood there waiting vainly for an answer.

'Good-night,' he said brokenly. 'I'll come again, when you've had time to think a bit. I do you justice. I've thought an' said a hunderd times to-day as if annybody had brought a charge like that agen me, I'd never ha' spoke to him, not if he was dyin'. I know it's hard ; but you'll forgive me in the long-run, an' I'll—I'll leave you for a bit to think it over. Good-night, my lad, an' bless you always.'

He lingered for a while ; and then, finding me still obdurate, went away through the open doors; and I heard him pass down-stairs, and listened to his steps until they died upon the gravel of the pathway in the square. Then my shame and pity ran in upon me in an agony, and I would have given all I had to recall the last five minutes. But I told myself that the chance of reconciliation was gone, and stayed where I was, and nursed my miseries, and justified myself in my own mean mind, and bolstered the shameful purpose I had held to with spites and prides : and through it all suffered, I hope, as I deserved to suffer.

Uncle Ben came no more : but Will and Maud called upon me on their return from the continent, and begged me to be reconciled. I besought them in turn to leave that theme alone : but at last Maud drew from me the reason of my refusal, which indeed she had guessed all through.

'You shall come with me to Uncle Ben,' she said ; 'and neither of you shall say a word about it, but you shall be friends. "Let the dead past bury its dead," my dear.—Do you know who is with us at the Langham ? —No ? Your cousin Mary. You must let us take you back. You know,' she said, speaking apart to me, while Cousin Will stood outside smoking his cigar upon the landing-place, and taking an intense interest in the balustrades—'you know that Mr. Fairholt's objections are likely to endure as long as your enmity to Uncle Ben.'

'There again,' I answered, 'you urge me to my own ·advantage. I must forgive a wrong to profit by forgiveness. You make it harder for me—not easier.'

'It is now four o'clock,' said Maud, ignoring my pride and my pettishness, 'and we have purchases to make. We will call for you at six. You will come, I know,' she said : and added sweetly, 'You can make us all happy. Come.'

I promised to answer her when she came again ; and I accompanied them to the gates, and saw them drive away. Not knowing what to do with the two hours which were thus left on my hands, I rambled into Chancery Lane thinking, and determining more and more to ask Uncle Ben's forgiveness in my turn. Moved by this growing resolve, I walked faster and faster, along Holborn and into Oxford Street, and was pushing on at a great pace, when a shabby, panting, breathless creature ran full tilt against me, and in the mutual recoil and stare, the man Penkridge and I recognised each other. I was going by, when, with wheezing haste, he besought me to stop a moment.

'What is it?' I said, a little angrily.

'Ho, sir,' he panted, 'no doctor as don't know me'll think o' comin',' sir, for a cove like me. But the poor Duke, he's a dying, sir, an' Mr. Hastings he'd give anything to have him seen to proper. Oh sir, I've been for Dr. Brand, sir, an' he an't in, sir, an' I'm a-going to find the landlord, sir; an' would you, sir, for heaven's sake, go an' look at him?'

I tore a leaf from my pocket-book, and wrote upon it, 'An urgent case. Please, accompany messenger. I will be responsible for medical charges.' I signed this, and gave it to the man. 'Run with that to the nearest surgeon. Bring him to Bolter's Rents. I will go on and see if I can be of service.' I walked hurriedly to the Rents, mounted the creaking stair, and found the room, with half-a-dozen people jangling noisily in it about the bed. One old woman was burning feathers, and another held a basin of water in her hands. On the bed lay the recluse, a venerable figure, with long white hair and beard.

He was dressed, and lay motionless and unconscious, and there was a stain of blood upon
his silver head.

'What has happened?' I questioned.

The noise had ceased at my coming; and
one of the women answered in a whisper,
'Knocked down, sir, by a hansom. The
cabman's give up his ticket to the pleeceman,
sir.'

I ordered the burning feathers to be thrown
out of the window; and then felt the injured
man's pulse and examined his eye. He was
unconscious, and his pulse was feeble. I despatched one of the women for brandy, and
cleared the room of the others; and then
sitting by the bedside, awaited the arrival of
Penkridge and a doctor. I looked about the
bare and almost empty room, and then back
to the prostrate figure on the bed. The man's
face was calm, and had a venerable and even a
noble look; and I regarded it long and thoughtfully, for it seemed to stir in me a memory
of some one I had known long since. Looking away with abstract eyes, I saw a face
start from the whitewashed wall. I write of
my impression. There was no face in the
world I could less have expected to see limned

there than this—for it was Polly's. It was no fortuitous likeness, but a portrait, a reproduction in outline of the living face. It was but roughly traced in charcoal on the whitewash of the wall, but it was a master's work. Turning in a chaos of amazement, for which I can find no words, I saw above the low-browed fireplace a smaller sketch in pencil. Nearing this, I stood rooted before the almost living forms and faces of Will and Maud. They stood before me arm-in-arm, and the door of a church was indicated behind them. I went back to the bed, and looked again upon the man who lay there. The likeness I had dimly thought was there flashed out upon me. It was that of my Cousin Will—a resemblance disguised by the form and colour of the hair and beard, but growing more authentic to me every second. In my agitation I scarcely knew that I spoke aloud: 'Frank Fairholt did not die in the Crimea. This is he!'

The man's eyelids moved, and the eyes looked out from under the black eyebrows wearily, as though they surveyed some misery grown familiar. And I knew him then, beyond all chance of doubt, for the dreadful stranger of my childhood's dreams.

CHAPTER XIII.

' It is all atoned for ; but the atonement was not mine.'

I SAT beside the injured man, so marvellously discovered ; and as my mind grew calmer, I surveyed the chain of circumstance which led me there, and heaped surmise on surmise as I strove to guess what hideous compulsory fate had driven such a man as Frank Fairholt had been to such a place as this. When Penkridge came at last accompanied by a surgeon, I waited only to carry away a sounder opinion of the medical aspect of the case than I could form. I had already given the patient a little brandy, and had moistened his lips and temples with the spirit ; and his pulse was somewhat accelerated when the surgeon came.

'I can have no opinion yet,' he said in

answer to my inquiry. ' He is an old man, and a shock of this kind may prove fatal.'

' Will you be good enough to remain with him ? ' I asked. ' I will drive to Dr. Brand, and either bring him back or leave word for him to come.'

' Dr. Brand ? ' said the surgeon. ' Do you mean *the* Dr. Brand ? of Wimpole Street ?

' He has taken a great interest in this man,' I answered, not caring to give either Penkridge or the surgeon any insight into my discovery ; ' and he will be glad to come.'

' I'm afraid the poor fellow will be scarcely able to pay Dr. Brand's fees,' said the surgeon.

' I will be answerable for that,' I returned ; and at once sped in pursuit of the doctor, whom I found in the act of sitting down to dinner. I told him hastily what I knew ; and he snatched up his hat and ran to the cab in haste. As we rode over the brief space between Wimpole Street and Bolter's Rents, he said only, ' Whether this extraordinary belief of yours be true or false, Campbell, there is a mystery about this man which may be unravelled now.'

' You know my cousin and his wife ? ' I asked ; and he nodded in reply. ' Look,' I added, 'at their portraits in pencil on his wall.'

He nodded gravely once more ; and neither of us spoke again until we reached the room. The surgeon met him with marked respect, and made some observation on the condition of the patient, which Dr. Brand disregarded. By what intuition he knew, I cannot tell, but the physician shook his head as he looked at the prone figure, and after the briefest examination, laid the patient's lax hand gently down. 'He will probably rally in four-and-twenty hours by the exhibition of cordials,' he said in a low tone to the surgeon ; 'but re-covery is impossible.'

The surgeon bowed assent to this judg-ment ; and the physician turned silently, and guided by my glance, walked to the fireplace and looked at the drawing above it. Guided by my glance again, he crossed the room, and looked at the drawing on the opposite wall. He said nothing then ; but after care-fully surveying the face, and standing before it thoughtfully a moment, he produced his pocket-book, and wrote out a prescription.

'This is a case,' he said to the surgeon, 'in which I take a deep and special interest.

Can you oblige me by securing a good nurse? We must do what we can for him, poor fellow;' glancing to the bed. The surgeon responding that he was happy to be of service, took his leave; and Dr. Brand, holding him a moment by the buttonhole, asked him to return at his earliest convenience. This he promised; and a minute later, Penkridge having been dismissed, the doctor and I stood side by side, looking down on the unconscious figure. 'Tell me,' he said in a low voice, 'on what you base your belief about this man's identity.'

In the same tone, I sketched the story rapidly; and the doctor nodded here and there to signify attention. 'These,' he said, waving his hand towards the sketches on the wall, 'are potent proof, certainly; but we shall probably know all when the patient rallies. It will be strange and terrible,' he murmured, 'if such a tragedy has been near us all these years, and we have never guessed it.'

'My Cousin Will is in town,' I reminded him, 'with his wife. My uncle is with them. It must be told to one of them. But Maud should never hear of it.'

'No,' he answered. 'I remember the story

well. They were lovers. We must spare her, if we can. Wait until the surgeon returns, and then find Mr. Hartley, and tell him what you believe. Let him be here before this hour to-morrow.'

I promised; and Dr. Brand departed. I waited until the darkness fell upon me, and I could see only the faint silvery gleam of head and beard as I looked upon the bed. And in the solemn silence, broken only by the breathing of the dying man, and by the roll of traffic, which sounded there like a murmur from the shore heard far inland, the better thoughts which had long struggled within me had full sway. I called to mind all the suffering which I had known to spring from the one tragedy whose end was drawing near so swiftly; and I vowed within myself that the hearts which had been so wounded, should henceforth know no added pang through me.

When at last my watch was over, and I had seen the nurse take her place, I betook myself to the Langham and asked for Uncle Ben. I discovered that he had not been told of Maud's attempt to persuade me, and that he had gone out to a dinner of some City magnates, with whom he had been associated in his business days.

But Maud and her husband and Polly were there, spending a restful evening in quiet talk. I told them of my better purpose with regard to Uncle Ben, and shrived myself of my ingratitude and hardness. And all the time, as Will and Maud talked happily, and as I read in every glance that passed between them, and in every tone as they addressed each other, their settled surety in each other's love ; and when I saw in Maud's dear face the placid happiness that beautified it, my thoughts turned back to the dying man who lay in the mean chamber so near at hand, and I thanked God that the two scenes were so wide apart in spite of nearness. It was after midnight when Uncle Ben returned, and Will and I were then alone. He came in with a sad and weary look, which touched me to the heart. He did not see me at first, and started at my voice.

'Uncle,' I said, 'I have acted vilely, and I am here to ask your pardon.'

He made no answer in words ; but coming near me, he placed his arms about my neck, as he had done when I was a child, and kissed me. Then with eyes a little dimmed, we shook hands heartily, and our reconciliation was complete. Will bade us both a cheery good-night,

and left us ; and then I told my story. It was
listened to with such wonder as may be ima-
gined ; and my uncle, much perturbed by it,
promised to be with me before noon, and to
accompany me to Bolter's Rents ; reserving
until after his visit, all opinion as to whether
Will should know of the belief at which I had
arrived. We met at the appointed time, and
walked to Oxford Street together.

'I have told Will privately,' said my uncle
as we went, 'that in two hours' time I *may*
want to see him on a matter of great importance ; and he's promised to wait for me.'

I understood from this that he had decided, in case he shared in my belief, to com-
municate the facts to Will ; and it seemed
to me that it was scarcely possible to do
otherwise. I had warned him of the nurse's
presence : and when we reached the room, I
pointed without comment to the sketches on
the walls ; and he stood before them in deep
amazement. Then after long and careful
study of the face of the dying man, he
beckoned me, and left the room on tiptoe.
When we reached the court, he turned an
agitated countenance upon me. ' There's
nothin' surer in the world, Johnny,' he said,

with tremulous solemnity. ' It's the man. I should ha' known him in a crowd, if I'd had reason to look at him.'

' Mr. Hastings saw him,' I returned, ' when he was probably less changed than he is now, and did not know him.'

' Yes,' assented my uncle; ' but Hastings didn't have the pictures to guide him; and he thought he'd buried him 'ears an' 'ears ago, in the Crimea.'

My uncle's disturbance was so evident, that I would not allow him to enter the hotel. We appointed a meeting-place; and I proceeded to the hotel alone, and sent a waiter to say that Mr. Hartley would be glad to see Mr. Fairholt at once. In a short time Will came down, and in some surprise set out with me. He asked in vain for an explanation; and we drove to Bolter's Rents in silence. There was a little crowd in the court waiting with anxious looks for news. Penkridge formed one of this sad knot; and touching his hat to me, humbly said that the nurse had left the patient for a time. He had recovered consciousness, and had asked to see a minister of religion. A priest who had within the last two or three months been in the habit of visiting the Rents, had been there at the time, and was now with him. I could not even yet bear to break the whole news to my Cousin Will ; but I said to him as we walked towards the end of the court, 'We have what I am afraid will prove a terrible surprise for you. We would have spared you if we could ; but we did not think it possible or right, and we have acted for the best.'

My uncle nodded in confirmation of my words, and held out a hand, warning us to silence as we reached the foot of the stairs. Slowly and silently, we climbed storey after storey until we reached the last flight, when we heard the sound of a measured voice reading. As we stood, we could even hear the words which told the parable of the Prodigal Son. At a further gesture from my uncle's hand, we went on silently, and paused upon the landing. There Will laid a hand upon my arm ; and in the light which reached us through the half-open door, I saw his lips shape a word—a name. I nodded, in token that I knew it ; and we stood in silence. Another voice spoke in repetition of the immortal words—' BUT WHEN HE WAS YET A GREAT WAY OFF, HIS FATHER SAW HIM.'

Will Fairholt's face turned ghastly pale; and like one who had no power or will to stand or stay, but moving as though another mind impelled him, he passed into the room. We who remained without with beating hearts, heard on a sudden a wailing cry, and silence fell, broken after a space by sobs and murmurs.

'Will,' said the voice which had spoken last, 'God is merciful. It is all atoned for; but—the atonement—was not—mine.'

A sigh followed; and there came another silence, and then Will's voice called upon his brother: 'Frank! Frank! Look at me! Speak to me!'

There was no sound of answer; and when we dared at last to enter the room, we saw the brother a second time bereaved, upon his knees beside the bed, with his face lying on the dead man's outstretched hand. And in the open eyes from which the glory of the prophecy of death had not yet faded, there was peace unspeakable.

There was one in the garb of a friar who stood beside the bed with downcast eyes, whom all the living there had known and loved, whom we could know and love no longer. And after a while he went his way with downcast eyes and bitter tears; and there was no word spoken and no sign made among us.

We drew poor Will away gently, and sent the nurse to her last melancholy function. And whilst Will was weeping for his brother, Hastings came and learned the story, and was smitten with grief and wonder. But when we were all a little stronger, we made a solemn pact that our knowledge should rest among us; and only we four, and Dr. Brand, know upon whose grave the flowers bloom so sweet in the quiet churchyard near Frank Fairholt's ancient home.

THE END.